The Cotter's Son

A Story From Sigdal

The Cotter's Son   (Husmannsgutten)
A Story From Sigdal
By H.A. Foss
English Translation by Joel G. Winkjer
Preface and Afterword by Andrea Winkjer Collin

English translation Copyright 1962
by Joel G. Winkjer

Preface and Afterword Copyright 1998
by Smoky Water Press

Printed in the United States of America

1   2   3   4   5   6   7   8   9   10   11   12   13

ISBN   0-9644389-4-1

Cover design by Brian Austin
Mandan, North Dakota

The Cotter's Son:
A Story From Sigdal

Husmannsgutten:
En Fortelling Fra Sigdal

By
H.A. Foss (1884)

Translation By
Joel G. Winkjer (1962)

Smoky Water Press
Bismarck, North Dakota
USA

Also available from Smoky Water Press

Bloody Knife: Custer's Favorite Scout By Ben Innis, edited by Richard E. Collin. The only book-length biography of the Arikara Indian scout who died with Custer at the Battle of the Little Bighorn. Features maps, 65 photographs, including a previously unpublished photograph of Custer, new preface written by a descendent of Bloody Knife and an appendix of all Indian Wars battles. 320 pages. $18.95 softcover. ISBN 0-9644389-0-9

Bloody Knife: Custer's Favorite Scout By Ben Innis, edited and narrated by Richard E. Collin. Book-on-tape, three hours. $14.95 ISBN 0-9644389-1-7

The Search For Common Ground In Sex Education By Ed Crawford, M.A. The long-time director of the Eckert Youth Homes of Williston, North Dakota, shares his experiences with helping "at risk" youth develop "conscience-equipping skills," and presents "ten essentials" for groups to adopt when establishing community sex education programs. 90 pages, $9.95 softcover. ISBN 0-9644389-2-5

Falling Between the Cracks By Avis Dissell. The inspirational story of a woman who has spent twenty-five years helping her husband recover from and cope with a serious traumatic brain injury. 140 pages, $12.95 softcover. ISBN 0-9644389-3-3

Following The Custer Trail of 1876 By Laudie Chorne. This day-by-day account traces the exact route between May 17 and June 25, 1876, when Lt. Col. George Custer marched his Seventh Cavalry from Fort Abraham Lincoln, Dakota Territory, to the banks of the Little Bighorn River, Montana Territory, to fight America's most famous Indian Wars battle. 200 pages, $34.95 hard cover, $19.95 softcover. ISBN 0-9644389-5-X

Send check or money order to **Smoky Water Press, P.O. Box 2322, Bismarck, ND 58502-2322.** *For shipping and handling add $2 for the first book and $1 for each additional. North Dakota residents add sales tax.*

701-222-0941

Andrea Collin

Contents

Preface

My interest in republishing the English translation of this popular Norwegian-American novel comes naturally, given my heritage as an American "baby boomer" whose ancestors all came from Norway. I grew up enjoying family stories about the Winkjers and Helles from Trondhjem, the Sondreaals and Stolens from Hallingdal, the Septons and Olsens from Oslo and the Carlsons and Farlands from Stavanger.

The stories ... Great Grandpa Gunnar Winkjer's year-long gold mining adventure in Australia and New Zealand, which produced a gold nugget that a London goldsmith made into the wedding ring now worn by my mother for nearly fifty years ... the Helle family whose hometown near Trondhjem was actually named Hell! ... Great Grandpa Torkel Farland, the sea captain who sailed emigrants between Stavanger and New York City ... Great-Great Grandpa Ole Olsen, a penitentiary guard in Oslo ... so many stories!

Like those passed down from generation to generation in all families, these stories, had their details been preserved, would have rivaled any fiction penned by a novelist like Hans Andersen Foss.

I have taken on this project not as a Scandinavian

scholar, but as someone who has fostered a lifelong interest in my Norse heritage. For a few weeks during the summers of 1964 and 1965 I was a resident of Skogfjorden, the Norwegian language camp sponsored by Concordia College of Moorhead, Minnesota. I studied Norwegian at the University of North Dakota for two years in the 1970s, and I visited Norway twice, in 1970 and 1975. On the first trip I was a member of a high school band of young people from North Dakota's Williams County that marched in parades celebrating the City of Bergen's 900th anniversary. The second visit was as a journalism student in college. *The Williston Herald*, my hometown newspaper, asked me to cover a trip by another county-wide group to celebrate the Bicentennial of the United States in Norway. It worked out that I could leave for Norway a few weeks early and take part in a study tour of the country led by my university Norwegian instructor, Arne Brekke.

Twenty-five years have not dimmed the vividness of these memories. In the years since I have sustained an interest in my Scandinavian heritage and in how this heritage has influenced the American I am today.

H.A. Foss's story, *The Cotter's Son*, has been a part of my family since the mid-1880s, when my ancestors who were already in America read the story as a serial in the *Decorah-Posten*, one of many Norwegian language newspapers published in the country. In 1962, my great-uncle, Joel Winkjer, who first read it as a teenager at his home in Minnesota, completed the translation of this story. The following year it was published by the Park Region Publishing Company of Alexandria, Minnesota.

Throughout my family there was not a little excitement over this book coming out. Then a fourth grader, I took on the challenge of reading the book, enjoying the story of Ole and Marie, and appreciating a bit more the stories about my own ancestors.

I especially felt an empathy with the characters in the story whose names were the same as some of my own ancestors -- Ole, Marie, Torkil, Carl and Einar. And Ole's emigration experience and homesteading struggles on America's prairies struck a familiar chord as well. The countryside of northwestern North Dakota was then still dotted with tiny abandoned shacks that were home to homesteaders barely a generation before, including two great grandparents and a grandfather, Andrea Carlson Farland, Even E. Septon and Jonathan Winkjer.

As a nine-year-old reading this story for the first time in 1963, I imagined that many of Ole's sterling qualities were shared by some of my family members who immigrated to the same part of America as he did. Especially vivid is the photograph in our family collection of the six Winkjer sons of East Moe Township, Douglas County, Minnesota in 1914. Pictured were Great Uncle Joel, the translator of this book, Great Uncle Theodore, who helped Joel with publishing arrangements of this book in 1963, and my grandfather, Jonathan, who at six feet, two-and-a-half inches tall, was the shortest of the brothers!

While always commanding a place of prominence on my family's bookshelves, it wasn't until after I began a publishing company in 1994 that I took a

The Cotter's Son

renewed interest in republishing this book and making it available to another generation of Norwegian-Americans.

With the blessing of Great Uncle Joel's granddaughter, my second cousin Virginia Brown, and her children, Russell Brown and Laura Jeffrey, I have savored this project. Especially rewarding has been the additional research that led to new information about and a greater appreciation for both H.A. Foss and Joel G. Winkjer. As a native North Dakotan who has spent most of her life in the state, I am proud that Foss called this state his home for thirty years.

I have been intrigued with the impact *The Cotter's Son* has had on more than a century of Norwegian readers. The most recent publication of the book in 1984 marked its sixteenth printing in the country, and contains an interesting afterword by Nordic literature scholar Liv Kristin Asheim. She is one of several Norwegians who have written about *The Cotter's Son* and the impact Foss's story had on creating a greater awareness of the injustice of the cotter's system that then prevailed throughout Europe. Asheim compares *The Cotter's Son* to Harriet Beecher Stowe's *Uncle Tom's Cabin*, a popular literature book first published in 1852 that brought a greater awareness of the injustice of slavery in America.

The Norwegian I learned at Skogfjorden and at the University of North Dakota, and which has been lodging dormant in a convolution of my brain for more than two decades, was called into service once again as I tackled the translation of Asheim's article. This was done with the help of Einar Haugen's Norwegian-English dictionary, which I've carried since college, and even more so through the help of a new friend, Tone-Lise Stenslie, a native of Voss, Norway, who now lives in Mandan, North Dakota. She made sense of those phrases that only someone fluent in the language can interpret.

Along with this is another interesting article about Foss we translated, written by the late Norwegian author and journalist Oddmund Ljone and published in the *Nordmanns-Forbundet Magazine* in January 1952, shortly after the centennial of Foss's birth in November 1951.

I believe these writings should be read only after readers enjoy Foss's novel. That is where I am also including the additional information about Foss that I have gathered and which is not covered by Asheim and Ljone.

But first, readers should let the story of *The Cotter's Son* transport them back to Norway's Sigdal Valley of the mid-1800s and to America's promised lands in Wisconsin and Illinois. This enduring story of love, faithfulness and devotion rings as true today as it did 115 years ago.

Andrea Winkjer Collin
September 1998
Bismarck, North Dakota
USA

Acknowledgments

Republishing this book has only been accomplished with encouragement and guidance from many individuals, whom I will attempt to inclusively acknowledge here.

At the top of the list is the family of Joel G. Winkjer, his granddaughter, my second cousin Virginia DeAtley Brown, Bethesda, Maryland, and her children, Russell Brown of Rome, New York, and Laura Jeffrey of Rockville, Maryland. They gave their blessing to this effort and shared information, insight and enthusiasm. I sincerely thank them.

The research skills of many professionals helped uncover additional material for the introductory pages. My appreciation goes to: the staff of the State Historical Society of North Dakota in Bismarck, including Lotte Bailey, deputy state archivist and especially Susan Dingle, reference specialist; Dina Tolfsby, editor of *The Norseman* magazine at Nordmanns-Forbundet in Oslo; Carolyn Twingley at the Bismarck State College Library; the Orin G. Libby Special Collection staff at the University of North Dakota Chester Fritz Library in Grand Forks; Debbie Sandvold, librarian at the *Minot Daily News*, Jeannie Narum of the Minot Public Library, Jim and Florence Johnson, and Allen Larson at Creative Media, all of Minot, North Dakota; Reverend Arland Fiske, formerly of Minot, now Laporte, Minnesota; Carol Hasvold, registrar and librarian at the Vesterheim Museum and Jane Kemp, director of circulation and special collections, and Rachel Vagts, archivist, from the Preus Library at Luther College, all of Decorah, Iowa, and Barbara Grover, director of the Douglas County Historical Society, Alexandria, Minnesota.

Peter and Tone-Lise Stenslie, Mandan, North Dakota, gave assistance in several ways, especially translating documents with expertise that far exceeds my limited proficiency in Norwegian. I appreciate the permission of artist Margaret Johnson, now of Denver, Colorado, to once again use the striking cover picture she painted for the 1963 edition. Brian Austin, Mandan, North Dakota, shared his graphic design talents to give this book a distinctive style. Several employees at Aschehoug & Co. Publishing Company in Oslo, worked with me to obtain permission to reprint Liv Kristin Asheim's article that appeared in their 1984 publication of the book. Dave Luyben, my valued colleague at Bismarck State College, and Jerry Anderson, my former colleague at the University of Mary, both of Bismarck, provided technical advice. Sandy Smith Ganje, my friend since high school, helped with typesetting, and her daughter, Valecia Ganje, offered her ever steady hand with three young girls whose mother had her nose in front of a computer screen for most of a summer.

Others whose information helped answer questions include: Gudbrand Haugen from the Cultural Affairs Office of the Norwegian Embassy in Washington, D.C.; John Haaven, general manager of the *Park Region Echo* newspaper and Margaret Luethner, both of Alexandria, Minnesota.

On a personal note, my family is due a note of appreciation for their support, advice and perseverance throughout this project; especially my mother and father, Betty and Dean Winkjer, Williston, North Dakota; my mother- and father-in-law, Genevieve and Everett Collin, Windom, Minnesota; my sisters and brother, DeAnn Allen, Early, Iowa; Kirsten Eppinger, Victoria, Texas; and Jonathan Winkjer, Harbor Springs, Michigan, and my sisters- and brothers-in law, Carol Kendrick, Columbia, Maryland; Mary McCormack, Arlington, Texas; Tom Collin, Cleveland, Ohio, and Dan Collin, Windom, Minnesota. To daughters, twins Sonja and Elizabeth, seven, and Karen, two, your mother enjoyed your company on our research and information-gathering trips around North Dakota, Minnesota and Iowa, even if you weren't exactly sure what they were about.

And, finally, to my husband Rick, my partner in parenting, publishing and everything in between, I appreciate all you have done to help me complete this project. While justified, you have never put the bumper sticker on your car that reads, *Pray for me. I am married to a Norwegian*. And, you have maintained a healthy respect for Norwegian traditions since, after digesting a Christmas Eve lutefisk dinner prepared by my grandmothers and mother in 1985, you were overcome with the inspiration to propose marriage to me. I am not a little happy you are part of my life, and I am not a little proud of all we have accomplished together.

AWC

Cover Artist

The cover depicts a scene from the book that was painted for its 1963 edition by artist Margaret Johnson. Born with multiple congenital deformities, she has had a successful career as an artist while confined to a wheelchair. A native of Holdrege, Nebraska, Margaret graduated from the Minneapolis Art Institute. She was a commercial artist at the *Park Region Echo* newspaper in Alexandria, Minnesota, when she illustrated a 1962 Kensington Runestone documentary comic book. When she painted *The Cotter's Son* cover, she worked at a Bismarck, North Dakota, advertising agency owned by Lloyd Omdahl, who was the state's lieutenant govenor from 1987-92. Margaret also lived in Fargo, North Dakota, and Rapid City, South Dakota, before moving to Denver, Colorado, in 1970. Since retiring, she teaches art classes and is involved in many senior activities.

Supporting Norwegian Studies

For every copy of *The Cotter's Son* sold, Smoky Water Press will make a contribution to the **University of North Dakota's Nordic Initiative Group.** This fund supports the state's only program that offers a major in Norwegian. Students achieve fluency in the language, study the history of Norwegian cultures and literature, pursue advanced degrees which draw on this background, and provide leadership in areas which connect Nordic countries with the United States. Other programs include a School of Law exchange with the University of Oslo and an undergraduate exchange with Ostfold Academy in Moss, Norway. For more information contact the UND Foundation, P.O. Box 8157, Grand Forks, ND 58202, phone 800-543-8764, 701-777-2611.

About the Translator
Joel G. Winkjer

After a twenty-five-year career as associate dairy husbandsman for the United States Department of Agriculture, Joel G. Winkjer retired at the end of 1940. He was a man of many talents and interests, including archery, ice skating, biking, horseshoe pitching, singing, dancing, horticulture, research, writing and cartooning. This made the quarter century of retirement until his death at age ninety-four in 1964 active and full. His height of six-feet five-and-a-half-inches, afforded him the distinction of portraying Uncle Sam in numerous Washington, D.C., parades.

Of exclusively Norwegian stock, Winkjer's parents came to America in 1864 from the Trondhjem area. They settled on a farm in East Moe Township, Douglas County, Minnesota, in 1868. Joel G. Winkjer was born to Gunnar T. and Karen Anna (Helle) Winkjer on December 31, 1870, the second oldest of eleven children. Seven of them lived to adulthood.

He grew up on the family farm, was educated in public schools and later attended the School of Agriculture at the University of Minnesota. While at the University, he played center on the football team in 1896 and 1897. He became the first manager of the Garfield, Minnesota, creamery, the town nearest his family's farm. After two additional years of special courses at the University of Minnesota, he became a creamery operator at Thief River Falls, Minnesota. Later he was appointed by Governor John A. Johnson creamery inspector for northern Minnesota, headquartered in Crookston. Governor Adolph Olson Eberhart appointed him Minnesota Dairy and Food Commissioner in 1909. He moved to Washington in 1915 to spend the rest of his professional career with the United States Department of Agriculture.

On August 7, 1898, Joel married Helga Elizabeth Eggen of Garfield, Minnesota, one of the county teachers at that time. They were married for sixty years and raised two children. Their daughter, the late Thelma DeAtley, was a teacher at Coolidge High School in Washington, D.C., and a painter who specialized in copying masterpieces at the National Gallery of Art. Their son, the late Guy Archibald Winkjer, was a patent attorney for Goodrich Rubber Company.

As he moved through his eighties and was forced to curtail some of his physical activities, his daughter

This 1914 photograph shows the six sons of Gunmar and Karen Anna Winkjer, who were raised in East Moe Township of Douglas County, Minnesota. From left, they are Theodore, Joel, Jonathan, Gideon, Kraft and Taulo.

and granddaughter suggested he translate Norwegian poetry into English. Having grown up speaking Norwegian at home, he knew the language well enough to enjoy doing this. He then got the idea to translate the H.A. Foss novel *Husmandsgutten*, which he had first read as a teenager. (When translated into the more modern dialect of Nynorsk in the 1950s, the title became *Husmannsgutten*.)

Why would a person of such advanced age take on such a project instead of slowing down? A clue is found in a June 1961 letter Winkjer wrote to Thompson Webb at the University of Wisconsin about his translation work: "It may be that I have informed you about my age before, but giving it as it stands now, I will have finished the first half of my ninetieth year the last day of this month. I am playing with this writing to delay my mind growing stale."

Driven to be as accurate as possible with the translation, Winkjer even traveled to Norway in 1960 at the age of eighty-nine. By coincidence, there he met a man he had not seen for seventy-five years, someone who had emigrated to America and worked on his uncle's farm for a few years before returning to Norway.

Two years after the trip to Norway, his granddaughter Virginia DeAtley Brown had typed and retyped page after page of his translation. His friend, Alfred Stefferud, the Department of Agriculture's chief editor who also was fluent in Norwegian, took on the task of reviewing Winkjer's translation. With Stefferud's blessing, the final translation was completed in 1962. His brother, Theodore, stepped forward to help with publishing arrangements with the Park Region Publishing Company of Alexandria, Minnesota, which put out the newspaper in the brothers' home county. The newspaper's publisher, Carl A. Wold, was a college classmate of Joel Winkjer's. Wold was also the son of Norwegian immigrants, and a popular Prohibitionist, Minnesota legislator and political progressive.

In the introduction to the 1963 publication of *The Cotter's Son*, Winkjer wrote about why translating this story interested him:

"Among the many things of interest in the story is the picture of a condition that had its influence on the migrations of Norwegians to the United States during the 1870s and 1880s. A poem written in Norwegian during this period (author unknown) expresses this situation; one verse of which is translated here into prose:

"Hail the land which God has planted into the lap of the world's ocean as a refuge for the poor and needy from the old world's wants. With a warm embrace she welcomes all comers of whatever tongue or rank. Her wide stretches invite with open arms to a home for you and yours.

"Although the immigrants used their native language while learning the English of the new homeland, their descendents have gradually lost the understanding of Norwegian and are closing the door to the information and entertainment so richly contained in Norwegian literature. The same conditions exist among people of other foreign extractions as all merge together in one nation and one language."

He also wrote that in Foss's novel, "family life, the

great struggle for existence, and the joy and sorrow of the main character, Ole Haugen, have such realism that many readers, including the translator, have found that their own lives ran parallel at many points with Ole's."

In a fourteen-page letter to his six-year-old grandson Russell Brown in 1956, Winkjer further explained why he took on this project. Here are excerpts:

Dear Russell,

As a teen-ager it was my opportunity to read "Husmandsgutten," a novel written in Norwegian by Hans Andersen Foss. After a period of 72 years, now, as an octogenarian, the privilege is again granted me. Recognizing an old friend, the thought came to me that this would be a very interesting and informative story for you to read since you have a goodly portion of Viking blood flowing through your veins. Although at your age the story is too difficult to read now, in a few years, however, you will be delighted to read about Ole, the cotter's son.

But then, Russell, this difficulty presented itself -- you cannot read Norwegian. You could learn that language, of course. Another way would be to translate the story into English. But you would not expect me to do all that for you, would you?

After thinking that matter of translating over, it became evident that there are hundreds of thousands of "Russells" and "Russellettes" of Norwegian descent who would like to read about their Norwegian kinfolk and the customs of the land in which they lived and the suffering and privations they experienced.

The book is an intimate life story of a family depicting

The Cotter's Son xv

the customs of people, many of whom migrated from Norway to America. And here, Russell, comes an interesting quirk in the situation. Norwegians, Swedes and Danes each have their own literature printed in their own style, but when translated into English the story is that of all Scandinavians who have made America their homeland. Yes, of all the foreign countries who sent emigrants to the United States, those countries especially had the same system of farm labor.

The story is a novel, but it is true to life. I know that because I was born in America and was brought up and pioneered with a Norwegian emigrant parent family in a Norwegian settlement.

Let me give this little incident of my opportunity to learn the Norwegian customs. The cotter in Norway at this time was obliged to show his servility to the Bonde (farmer) and his family by stepping aside when we met and doffing his hat. Father had a farm, probably twice as large as that of the Bonde in Norway, and we were not a little amused when the newcomer cotters, hired by Father, would doff their hats to us.

Reading the book, "The Cotter's Son," will give a correct picture of conditions that had their influence on the great migration which was at its peak during the period that the book was first printed.

It is evident that Scotland also had the same system of engaging the cotters for farm labor. It is described in Robert Burns's poem, "The Cotter's Saturday Night," a classic in literature. To a great extent the cotter and landowner relationship was prevalent all over Europe. Thus, "The Cotter's Son" translated becomes a source of interesting information to a vast number of descendents of emigrants to America. Its timeliness is indicated by its many reprints. Although this is an indication of popularity, one must remember this is a demand only from those who can read Norwegian, now a dwindling number, while the Norwegians who know only English are increasing. Reprinting in Norwegian may cease and the story lost. The translation will save its life. In my humble opinion it is a live bud well worthy of being grafted onto our American literature.

Joel G. Winkjer

Joel G. Winkjer dedicated the 1963 publication
of the English translation of this book
to the memory of the woman he called his
"steady" for sixty years, his wife,
Helga Elizabeth Eggen Winkjer
(1875 - 1956).

*This 1998 republication is dedicated
to the memory
of Joel and Helga's daughter,*
Thelma Winkjer DeAtley
(1904 - 1996).

*A school teacher, accomplished painter
and long-time swimming instructor,
Thelma inspired those who knew her
with her zest for life
and her passion for keeping the bonds strong
between a family that most of the time
distance kept far apart.*

The Cotter's Son

Husmannsgutten
NORWEGIAN and DANISH

Husmanspoiken
SWEDISH

Rengen Poika
FINNISH

Sonur Vinnumannsins
ICELANDIC

The larger farmers in Scandinavian and other European countries employed year 'round help to do the necessary farm work. They often hired a man to be a tenant farmer and live with his family in a separate house or cottage on that farm. He was referred to as a *husmann* in Norwegian, which translates to *cotter* in English. The words "cotter's son" are identical in meaning with "husmannsgutten."

Irish and Scotch peasants have also carried the name of Cotter.

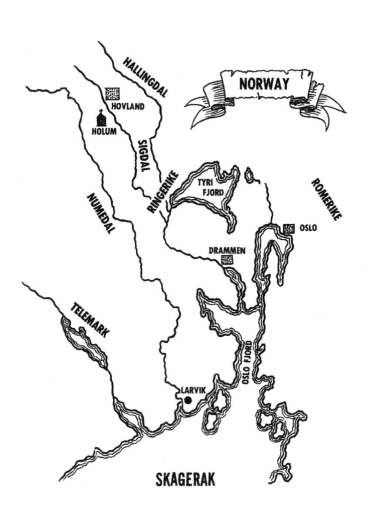

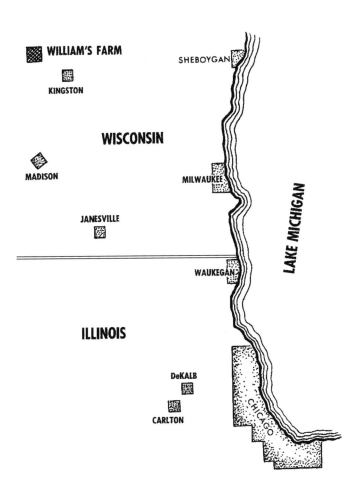

WILLIAM'S FARM

KINGSTON

SHEBOYGAN

WISCONSIN

MADISON

MILWAUKEE

JANESVILLE

WAUKEGAN

LAKE MICHIGAN

ILLINOIS

DeKALB

CARLTON

CHICAGO

Chapter One

The Cotter's Son
At His Master's Home

In the innermost parish of Sigdal Valley, Norway nestled the well known farm of Hovland. Its beautiful location upon a gentle slope by a mountain stream, with a large white home and red barns, surrounded by green birches and fruit trees, made so impressive an appearance that it was considered the most beautiful farm in the whole valley. Many vacationers came there from the city to rest. They often stayed for many weeks and found the fresh mountain air a source of strength for tired bodies and the surrounding scenery an inspiration for weary minds.

The owner was Torsten Pedersen Hovland, who inherited the estate from his father, Peder Torstensen. The Hovland farm had always been in comfortable financial circumstances.

It was springtime, a month before Easter, when Torsten's wife Gunhild, daughter of Sven Lie and bride of a year, gave birth to a daughter. There was a great to-do at Hovland those days. Folks came from north and south of the valley to bring the Hovland folks their congratulations and good wishes, accompanied by delicacies to eat and drink. Torsten Hovland was not a little proud of his daughter, and Gunhild not a little happy.

Wednesday before Maundy, when Gunhild was busy in the kitchen, Bonden (that is what they called all large land owners in Norway) came in smoking a long, ornate silver pipe and said to her, "The Haugen people will very likely bring their boy to baptism on Easter Sunday."

"I believe that's their intention," Gunhild answered. As she spoke, the kitchen door slowly opened and a tall, broad-shouldered, dark-complexioned man stepped in, a sheepskin cap in his hand.

He bowed deeply and said, "Good morning." Gunhild returned his greeting. He tossed his long black locks of hair out of his eyes as if he hesitated to state his errand, and all the while stood with downcast eyes, but suddenly he gained courage, lifted his head and looked at Bonden, to whom he said in a humble tone, "I am thinking of finding out if it were so that I could have twenty shillings today."

"What! Do you want money again?" was Bonden's blunt reply as a large cloud of smoke rose from his thick lips.

"Well, we are planning to have our boy baptized on Easter Sunday and so I'll need a few shillings for the minister and the sexton," said Torkil Haugen, the cotter on the farm, for he was the caller.

"Yes, you must have it, you say, but you will have to go elsewhere to get it, for you get nothing from me. You owe me enough now!" answered Bonden, becoming more vociferous. "I made up our account last week and found that you owe me exactly nine dollars, four marks, and nineteen and a half shillings, without counting the last oats you got. And still you can be insolent enough to come and ask me for money! No! Since you have been so stupid as to get married without the least concern about the future, or how you are going to support a family, you certainly cannot expect people to have sympathy for you and stand ready to hand out to you whatever you demand!"

Torkil was prepared for such a reception and was not too surprised, but he thought Bonden's remarks regarding his marriage were galling and he dared to answer, "Yes, maybe Randi and I, like other poor people, had a dark future for our marriage, but even if we lacked land we did not lack love. We put our faith in God and our good health."

"Yes, I have heard many like you say that they rely on God. On the other hand, I have never heard that This Man ever visited a poor man's cot or helped anyone," retorted Bonden in a derisive tone. "You will have to wait a long time before you get twenty shillings from Him," he added.

Torkil could see that it was useless to mention money again. He turned and put his hand on the door latch to depart when Bonden spoke to him again. "What have you been doing all week when you have not been seen here on the farm?"

"I have had to fetch home some firewood for the holy days."

"Wood! Have you already burned the wood you got for Christmas? How dare you go up in the forest and take wood I have not selected for you? Our contract allows you to have free fuel, but I did not intend to have you ruin the whole forest the first year! No, if you don't get home and bring every stick back to its place, I will show you where David bought his ale! And if you don't want to starve, it is best that you show up here on the third day of Easter and every working day after that. You must remember that it will take you twenty-six weeks of work to pay your debt, even though I pay you eight shillings a day when the cotter on the neighboring farm receives only six."

Before he had finished these words Torkil was on his way out.

Gunhild had listened with warm sympathy to all Torkil had to endure for making a desperate effort to obtain twenty shillings for such an important event as the baptism of his dear baby. She could not refrain from remarking to her husband, "These poor Haugen folk are not having it so good. Both of them are such good workers that given time now in the beginning, they will eventually clear themselves even if the debt was made a little larger. Summer will soon be here and then both can get some work on the side."

"Well, Gunhild, I'm not unreasonable,"

said Bonden, "and as fast as they earn it they will be paid. I shall certainly not withhold as much as a half-shilling from the Haugen folk or anyone else. But if I should dish out to them all that they ask for and be responsible for all their wants, then it would be useless to have a contract with the cotter. I know well that Haugen is not the best place for a man to get ahead, but then Torkil cannot say that I urged him into the deal. He came himself and told me he was going to get married and asked if he could have permission to build a cottage over there to live in. He was anxious to have a home, he said, and added that in time he could clear the stones from a piece of ground and plant potatoes. He thought that in this way he could manage, especially if he could get work on the farm. After we had agreed on the days throughout the year that he was obligated to work on the farm and because I considered him an able workman, I agreed to pay him two shillings more per day than my other hired men. Now you must understand, my dear wife, that I have done all I could for him and I do not mean to be hard on him; but I know that it is best for him to make both ends meet from the very beginning."

Gunhild knew that to say any more to Bonden would be like pouring water on a goose. As soon as he had gone into the living room she went to her bedroom and took a box from her bureau drawer. Then, unobserved, she went outside to meet Torkil and found him talking with Erick, the chore boy. She pressed a mark into his hands with these words, "It hurt me to hear the harsh answer Torsten gave you in reply to your small request, and I want you to know that I sympathize with you and your family. Take these twenty shillings which I have had since I was married, and with which I think I can do as I please. You may also have my savings bank which I got when I was a little girl. When you have the change for the mark, take four shillings and put it in and when the boy grows up you shall say to him that it is from me. Of course, you shall not bring back the wood, for Torsten has very likely forgotten it already."

Torkil was overjoyed, not only for the money but for the proof of Gunhild's sympathy and understanding of his plight. He put out his gnarled hand to thank her, but she was already on her way to the kitchen door. All he could do to make his gratitude known was to call after her saying, "God knows if I will ever be able to repay you for your kindness! If I can't, I hope that my boy will be able to!"

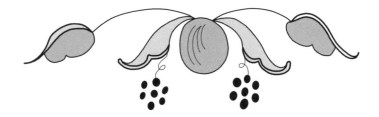

Chapter Two

Baptism of The Cotter's Son

Early Easter morning Torkil carried the baby boy in his arms and walked with Randi along the small path from Haugen towards the public road. There was a holiday manner in their walk, and their clothes too were different from everyday wear. Torkil had on his best suit, which had lain in the chest since his wedding day a year and a half ago. A black silk handkerchief nearly covered the collar of his clean but coarse gray linen shirt. Randi wore a black dress that looked as if it had been in existence in this world as many years as she herself. About her shoulders lay a shawl decorated with red blossoms that had belonged to her mother, Guri Svartbraaten. The road was good for walking and the weather beautiful, with birds singing and columns of golden sunbeams playing over the scene.

When they had walked quite awhile, Torkil suddenly pulled Randi aside and cried, "Look out! Get out of the way!" Just then the Hovland family sped by in their carriage, sitting comfortably wrapped under their bearskin robes as their horse, Blakken, trotted away with them over the smooth highway. Thore Viig and his wife, who had the farm next to Hovland, followed in their carriage and seemed to be well able to keep pace with their neighbors in equipment and in social arrogance.

"There is a great difference between people in this world," Torkil mumbled to himself. "Some live in luxury while others find it difficult to provide the bread they need."

"Yes, you are right about that," Randi answered, "But the world is not otherwise. We cannot all be rich, for then the farmers would not have anyone to thresh and winnow their grain. Or how do you think the farmers could pay their expenses if they did not have the cotters to chop their timber which they sell. No, then the trees would stand until they grew so large and old that no one could handle them. And another thing -- if we cotters' wives did not exist, then the whole country would have to go without socks, mittens, and linen shirts, for the farmers' wives must entertain ministers and businessmen and surely have their hands so full preparing food that they have no time to spin. No, we have each our definite calling and the assurance that we are of use among people. If we try to do our part faithfully, with prayer to God for strength, the work will be easy and performed happily."

"When you speak of threshing and logging I think you have gone into a subject you don't understand," Torkil remarked. "But when you go back to your own line of work of the spinning you are not so far out of line. From now on let us put such thoughts away from us and thank God for health. We can be just as happy in our cottage as the rich in their mansions."

As they went along talking while climbing the hill to the church, the bell tolled the second time, and Torkil asked Randi to hold their child so that he could remove his cap. This was customary in the valley when the church bell rang.

Randi carried the boy the remainder of the way to the church, and both entered, Torkil to seat himself on the men's side of the church, and Randi on the women's side. Torkil bowed and said his prayer, then he turned and hung his sheepskin cap on the wall. Looking around at the congregation he searched for the baby's sponsors and found his father-in-law, but the other, Tron Skaret, was not to be seen. "Tron has a long way to come from his out-of-the way place up the valley," Torkil reasoned, "and he cannot be expected to be on time."

Soon the last chime rang out over the valley and more people streamed into the church, but Tron was not among them. Prost Tandberg came out of the vestry and took his place by the altar as the old gray-haired Sexton Aas came forward to read the opening prayer. Next, he led the congregation in the singing of the hymn *Blessed Jesus, At Thy Word,* and each time the door opened Torkil turned to see if Tron were coming in.

When at last the Prost closed his sermon and the time for the baptism had come. Tron Skaret was still missing, and Torkil feared that he could not have his child baptized without two sponsors. Randi noticed her husband's look of distress and quietly went over to him, then shyly placed herself last in line where her mother was holding the baby boy. Mother Viig stood at the head of the row holding the Hovland daughter, and three beautifully dressed young women stood beside her as sponsors. On her other side stood three of the neighborhood's most important sons. Torkil had only himself and his father-in-law as sponsors, now that Tron Skaret had failed to come. These should surely be enough for a cotter's son, but he thought that even so he should talk to the sexton about it. He went over to him and whispered, "Tron Skaret, one of the sponsors I registered in the book, is not here. What shall I do?"

"Something had probably detained him," the sexton replied. "But be calm. I shall be a sponsor for your son in Tron's place."

Torkil was so delighted with this good luck that he nearly forgot he was in church. He took the three copper coins intended for Tron out of his pocket and offered them to the sexton, but Sexton Aas made a sign that this was not necessary. They walked down the aisle together to the end of the line.

The Hovland daughter was robed in a dress nearly four times longer than herself and trimmed with a profusion of little silk ribbons. She was named Marie after her grandmother, Marie Lie.

The cotter's son was clad in a simple little gown that had been borrowed from Berthe Skaret. He received the name Ole after his grandfather.

At the finish of the baptism, the Prost addressed the sponsors as "Good Christians," whether they were or not, and charged them with their responsibilities. A hymn was sung and the Prost took his place before the altar while each sponsor came up and presented money, half dollars from the Hovland party and copper shillings from the Torkil's little group.

After the Prost had chanted and hymns had been sung and Sexton Aas had given the benediction, nine strokes on the huge bell closed the services. Many relatives and friends gathered to go to Hovland, and Torkil's parents-in-law went to Haugen with the little family.

The next morning, the second day of Easter, when Torkil and Randi were eating their meager breakfast, they heard footsteps outside the door and Tron Skaret stepped in. He was dressed in his Sunday clothes and greeted them with a cheery "Good morning and Happy Easter!"

"Thanks, and the same to you!"

"But are you not ready yet?" Tron continued. "The sun is already way up!"

"Ready! We are going nowhere today."

"Was it not today you wanted me to come and be sponsor for your child, or were you just joking?"

"No, I said Easter Sunday! That's what I said. You know that there are no services in Holum church the second day of Easter!"

"What in the world!" exclaimed Tron. "Was it Easter Sunday yesterday? God forgive me, for I was in the woods chopping timber the whole day yesterday. Then also I have observed Maundy-Thursday on Friday and Good Friday on Saturday. Yes, and Palm Sunday on Monday. When one can't afford to spend six shillings for an almanac, poverty has gone too far. Now I have kept this same record of days since Thursday four weeks ago when I was at Berg's country store. We happened to mention in our talk that the date was the twenty-sixth of February and then I remembered that it was my Berthe's birthday. I asked Berg if he could not lend me a quarter pound of coffee so I could have something to treat the wife. This he did and when I came home I got some coffee ready. Berthe came in, and we sat and talked about this and that and, among other things, she told me she was born on Thursday. From that we have figured our dates."

"Yes, but you must know that if February twenty-sixth was on a Thursday thirty years ago, it might not be on a Thursday this year."

"But can that make a difference? I never knew that. Folks who live high up over the ridge as we do become as dumb as animals. But how did it go yesterday when I was not there? Did you have to go home without baptizing the baby?"

"Not at all, Sexton Aas was good enough to be sponsor in your place. He even refused to the offering, so now our boy already has ten shillings in his savings bank, let me tell you!"

"Well, you really must forgive me. Here is a pair of socks which Berthe sends as a christening gift. You must not refuse them."

There is a saying that "It is quick work to christen a cotter's boy." But that can hardly apply here, for Torkil had great difficulty in providing money, garments, and sponsors.

Chapter Three

The Farmer's Daughter And The Cotter's Son Are Playmates

The spring sun became warmer and warmer with each day and the snow had to yield its place to grass and flowers which covered the fields and meadows.

Torkil worked faithfully on the Hovland farm. In the spring Randi came with him, always bringing the little boy with her. From the time the haying began until the potatoes were dug late in the fall, she was there nearly every working day.

Mother Hovland, as Gunhild was always called, came to love the cotter's boy and it was she who gave him most care while Randi worked in the fields. She would often receive mild reprimands from her husband for attending to the cotter's son, but usually excused herself by telling him that it was not much trouble inasmuch as she had to take care of her own baby girl anyway.

"They play together," she said once, "and seem to know each other already."

"Hm-m," said Bonden, and wrinkling his forehead he took a deep draught from his pipe. As he turned to go back to the living room, he gave Gunhild a look as if to say, "You are making a mistake in treating them equally."

The babies were permitted to be together from one year to another and at last the relationship was taken for granted. Bonden and the farm people never gave it a thought. The cotter's boy was as much at home in the kitchen and living room as little Marie. That he slept during the night in the little hut at Haugen left little impression on the boy; for late at night after the day's work, when Randi took him home, she would find him in the cradle with Marie, the two lying side by side in sweetest slumber. And next morning, before his eyes were open, he was carried in his father's arms over to the farm, where he seldom awoke before he was again with his playmate.

Little children do not concern themselves

with matters of past or future, but should Ole ever have wondered about his home and family it would have been difficult for him to know whether he belonged to the farm or to the cotter's place.

From earliest childhood it was noticed that the cotter's son was very serious in whatever he undertook, and many a day Mother Hovland sat and observed the two playing on the floor. Ole was always the leader in everything, and Marie always joined in his impulses. Before they learned to talk they were like birds without words, understanding each other in a language all their own. One could hear Ole blabber something, and Marie would roly-poly over to the doll and bring it back.

So it went, one year after the other, and folks in the neighborhood thought that surely Mother Hovland planned to take the boy as her own. Very likely there was nothing she would have liked better if she could have had her own way, for Ole was now nearly as dear to her as her own Marie. He called her "Mama," but he feared Torsten and always called him "Bonden."

One day, in the middle of the summer, as Torsten sat in the parlor and conversed with visitors from the city, both the children came skipping in through the open door from the dining room.

"Two nice children you have. Are they twins?" asked one of the city folks as both were lifted up and caressed before Torsten could say anything.

"Only the girl is ours and she is a sweet little treasure. The boy is the son of one of the cotters and my wife is like a fool about him, dressing and caring for him like a farmer's son, although I have often called her attention to the unfortunate situation. Each should be brought up in his own environment and Ole will have to find out some time that as a cotter's son he will have to become used to something different."

"Well, I think he is altogether too good to be a cotter's son," remarked one of the guests and at the same time she pressed twelve shillings in Ole's small hand while he sat on her lap listening to all that was said. She kissed him on the cheek and let him down on the floor.

On the way home the same evening, Ole asked his parents if he could not stay at Hovland with Marie. This was something that they could not promise and he began to

The Cotter's Son

cry. Randi asked why he wanted to know, and Ole answered, "I heard Bonden say to the fine lady who gave me the money that I should find out something else; but may I be allowed to stay there if I stay in the kitchen Mama?"

"Oh yes," his mother replied. "Every working day you may stay there, but on Sundays you must be with me and help me."

The following spring Ole was five and a half years old. When he saw how the warm spring sun coaxed one blossom after the other out of the ground, saw the lambs gamboling in the meadows, now only sparsely covered with grass, and heard the cuckoo sing in the birches, then he was not content to stay in the kitchen and wanted to go outside. But he could not play without Marie, either. Then she was permitted to go out in the garden with him, and from that day on this was their favorite playground. There they could run about as they pleased for nature played no favorites; just as nice flowers grew on one spot as on another, and the roses were as lovely in one corner as in the other. How often did they know in their hearts the words of the Apostle Peter, "Here it is good to be." They built playhouses between the rose bushes, and one day after the other passed without either knowing any other grief than that of parting each evening. Ole would often hum this song he had learned from his mother:

> In morning time, where roses climb,
> I go so happily forth
> To pick the fragrant flowers
> And bind the garlands green
> To give my little friend.

> I Morgenstund til Rosenlund
> jeg gaar saa gjerne hen,
> plukker Blomsten skjon,
> binder Kransen gron,
> Til min lille Ven.

Chapter Four

The Cotter's Son Goes To The Mountain Pasture

Several years went by and Ole, in his eighth year, was ready to earn his own bread as a herder on the farm. That put an end to play and these two, as young as they were, had already lived the best days of their childhood. Ole, in his solitude on the grazing range, had abundant time to reflect and understand that he was only a cotter's son who had to adjust himself to other ways of life; especially when he had to stand in rain and sleet under the open heavens and often receive abusive reprimands from Bonden when, in closing darkness, he came home with the herd and a sheep or lamb was missing.

Ole was now large of body, bold and quick

to act, and had a manner of mind and countenance that revealed a seriousness seldom found in boys his age. Under the dark-brown curly locks of hair peered a pair of attractive bright eyes. His nose was slightly curved and well formed, and his mouth was set so that it definitely expressed the strength of will that lay behind it.

As soon as he had finished his breakfast each morning, he went over the knoll, driving the herd in front of him, straight as an officer leading a company of soldiers. Marie often stood in the farm yard and watched him and then stayed by the window as long as she could see him and the herd as they disappeared in the valley. Then she went up to her chamber where she could again glimpse Ole and the herd far off in the valley. On order, she would go to dinner, but rush back again to her vigil at the window. There she stayed from morning until night with apparent contentment.

This pleasure was not to continue for Marie, because as soon as there was grazing for the herd higher up in the mountains, Ole had to accompany Guri, the milkmaid, to the saeter* and he would not return until fall.

The lowly saeter life had a peculiar influence on Ole and laid the foundation for many of his ideas and observations. He had abundant time to speculate. Here his childish fantasy could leap from crag to crag, from lea to lea, and when he observed a peak in the distance he would say to Guri, who usually accompanied him, "I would like to know what is behind those mountains."

He learned to play the lur* and smiled to himself when the music was answered from the ridge. Then he would pretend it was the hulder* who answered him. But when, in the still evening, he called loudly, the voice returning would be so lovely that it could be none other than Marie's.

One day in October Marie stood up on a chair by her window the whole day and stared expectantly out over the saeter road which disappeared into the dark forest. Darkness had closed in, and although she was unable to see anything, she heard the tinkling of bells and soon the animals swarmed over the yard. Torsten Hovland was away that evening and Marie sat by Ole at the long table in the kitchen. The table sagged from the weight of the large bowls of steaming potatoes, surrounded by pans of milk and large bowl of herring. Ole told her the most important events that he had seen and heard during the summer, much to the interest of the listeners, after which Guri complimented him by saying, so all could hear, that he was as reliable as a grown man.

*LUR -- a musical wind-instrument similar to an elongated trumpet made from wood or birchbark or both, about 10 feet long and is played as a trumpet. The lur was used by the Budeier (dairy maids) in Norway when up in the *SAETER (mountain pasture) in summer to call the cows to their mountain home in the evening.

*HULDER -- a supernatural being, usually a woman; a mythical human being of folklore having diminutive form and magic power.

Chapter Five

The Two As Schoolmates

The following winter Ole and Marie began attending school. It was a good quarter of a mile to the school and Mother Hovland took the horse and drove Marie over there the first day. Ole, who now lived at home at Haugen, accompanied Asle Viig and other neighbor boys and girls. Asle outweighed Ole and had finer clothes, and he slyly suggested his imagined advantage by saying, "So you have corns on your toes, Ole? I see you have made a hole in your shoe."

The other children laughingly joined in the teasing that Asle had started.

"No, such holes make themselves," retorted Ole, and just then they heard a woman say, "Come, Ole. Have a ride with us!"

Ole did not hesitate to accept the invitation. But Asle, who would have begrudged him anything, threw a snowball at Ole, hitting him on his back as he drove away. From that day on the two were not good friends.

When Mother Hovland stopped at the schoolhouse, old Sexton Aas come out and tied the horse. After the greetings of the day and season she said smilingly, "Well, here I am with the twins. It is time that they should begin their schooling."

"Yes, in God's name, let them come! I shall care for them as if they were my own children. I have been sponsor for Ole. He is already a nice, big boy, I see!"

"Yes, and just as kind as he is nice. My sympathy has been with him since he was six months when he came with his mother to our farm. There was always something good about him."

It was time for opening the school. A hymn was sung, then the schoolmaster said a prayer. He prayed among other things that those who were placed in his care also would be led by the Fatherly Hand to that goal which is set in the school's curriculum.

Thereafter Ole went to school every other day, and the days between he spent in chopping wood for his mother, while his father worked on the farm each day.

For Christmas he received two very welcome presents: an iron-runner sled from his grandfather, Peder Svartbraaten, and a sister, born on Little Christmas Eve. Both made him very happy, but the sled was most attractive. He polished it and tried it out on the Haugen hill during the Christmas holidays, and when school began after New Year's he was not slow to challenge anyone to a race.

Asle Viig had a fine blue sled which proved to be no faster than Ole's. One morning Asle wanted Marie to ride with him on his sled down the Lie hill, but she declined saying, "I would rather walk." Then as Asle went down Ole arrived and Marie threw herself merrily in his lap and off they flew down the hill.

"I see that you would rather ride in the lap of 'Rag-Ole'," Asle teased as they met down in the valley.

There was little food at Haugen those days because the barrel of oats they had brought to the mill the week before had not yet been ground. Potatoes and bits of herring were divided between mother and son for breakfast.

"You must stay home from school today,

The Cotter's Son 29

my boy," said his mother regretfully while they were eating. "I have no food to send with you today."

"Oh shucks! That does not matter for a day if that is all," Ole answered cheerfully.

It was hard to send him off without food, but reluctantly she let him go.

At recess Ole found himself in a pinch which he had not thought of until then. What should he do when the others saw that he had no lunch along? He was unwilling to tell the truth, nor would he tell a lie. So he slipped out through the door when the others took their lunches and went behind the schoolhouse to sit quite depressed on his sled.

Marie noticed that he went out, and when he did not come back she suspected something was wrong and went to find him. She discovered him sitting back of the school writing the name "MARIE" in the snow.

"But why don't you eat, Ole?" she asked.

"I have no lunch with me today, but say nothing about it so that Asle Viig hears it, or he will get something to chew on again."

"I always have too much in my lunch and always have some left," Marie said. She offered him a sandwich and sat down on the sled beside him. The food tasted good, not only because it was much finer bread than he was used to, but because it was handed to him by Marie. After such a slim breakfast he was ravenously hungry.

Before Ole finished eating, the other children came out to play in the snow, making so much noise that the schoolhouse rattled. Asle saw the tracks in the snow and knew right away the two friends were together behind the building. He made a large hard snowball, edged himself along the wall to the corner and threw the ball with all his might. It was intended for Ole but it missed him and hit Marie right on the cheek. Her cheek swelled and flushed red as blood. Ole was so furious he could hardly control himself, but had enough presence of mind to lead Marie into the schoolhouse.

"Who threw that snowball?" he asked when he came out again.

"It was Asle Viig," said Guttorm Snaret, noticing the anger flashing from Ole's eyes.

"He shall not have done this for nothing," said Ole, "and before he gets home tonight he shall look like 'Rag-Asle' as surely as he called me 'Rag-Ole' this morning."

Recess was over and Sexton Aas called in the school children.

"What is the matter with you, Marie?" he asked and looked at the swollen cheek. She began to cry without answering and Ole was asked if he knew.

"A snowball hit her," said Ole.

"Who threw it?"

"I did not see, but the others say it was Asle Viig."

"I saw it! I saw it!" was heard from all sides.

Asle had to come forth to be questioned. He thought he could get out of it by saying that it was not meant to hit Marie, but rather was intended for Ole, in fun. However, the sexton was not going to be lenient because the ball was directed toward the cotter's son. He gave him three hard blows and placed him before the other school children, with a stick of wood in his mouth the whole afternoon.

On the way home Asle launched plans for revenge aimed at Ole, who first dared to tattle to the teacher. He began right away to tease Ole and asked if he left his oatmeal pancake home that morning.

"Oatmeal pancakes are not the best, but for a rich farmer's son to be gnawing on a dry stick of wood surely is not too good!" Ole retorted.

This was too much for Asle and he flew at Ole. A rough scuffle followed, which ended with Asle underneath and Ole sitting on top of him, in the ditch. Asle dragged himself home, his new blue shirt torn off and the other children crying, "Now you are 'Rag-Asle'."

But he declared that his father could lick the whole pack of Haugens.

Ole progressed rapidly in school in all subjects and became a good friend of the teacher, who understood that the boy was very gifted.

When spring came he had to quit school, for again he had to go to the saeter, and thus the years passed -- the saeter in the summer and school in winter.

Chapter Six

Christmas At Bonden's

Four years later, on Little Christmas Eve, Torkil and Randi sat talking about who should go because they had just received a half-barrel of oats and had no more coming.

The summer before Randi gave birth to twins, a boy and a girl, and now she had three small ones to take care of, which prevented her from doing any work on the farm. So Torkil was alone to earn the bread for himself and family and he found that eight shillings a day, which Bonden maintained was good payment, was very meager. There were twelve weeks each year when he worked without pay as rent for the plot of land on which his cot stood, but the poor soil gave him small return.

"I'm not afraid to go," said Ole. "I can't

fare any worse than to get a 'No!' for an answer."

"Well, we can wait until tomorrow," his father said, "And then you must tell him that we cannot get the oats ground in time for Christmas. Also, talk to him in as courteous a manner as you can."

Early the next morning the cotter's boy, now in his thirteenth year, stood in the kitchen at Hovland. Bonden was sent for and meanwhile Ole got a secret opportunity to press Marie's hand.

Presently Bonden came, broad and important, into the sitting-room and Ole, who no longer shook in his presence, asked him if he could have a bismerpund* of flour and a mark in money for coffee and sugar.

"It is likely wheat flour you want! Coffee and sugar, indeed! No, I really believe it is you who should move over here, and I go over to Haugen to live, for now it looks as if you are living more elegantly over there than we can afford here. I did not drink coffee before I was twenty-five years old and yet I did not die. You got a half-barrel of oats here a day or two ago, so I think it is best you start chewing on that and shut up."

"But we can't get it ground before

Christmas."

"I have not contracted to have the grain ground for you. Torkil could have brought the grain to the mill before. Let this be a lesson for another time. Furthermore, he cannot expect anything but poverty when he arranges it so that the woman has to lie home and care for little whelps. She did not think one was enough the first time, so now she brought two. But I hear that people brag that you are so good at school, and on the road from school -- both to read and tear the clothes off folks -- so likely you are able to find a way out for them, I should think.

"Rather than crawl and beg from you, I shall do all in my power to find some other way out," said Ole as his lips tightened.

"You dare to answer grown-ups too, you scamp! I shall see that you get out through that door!" shouted Bonden, evidently influenced by too much liquor in welcoming Christmas. He raced across the floor and tried to get the cotter's son by the collar and kick him, but the boy turned around and grabbed fast and sure the outstretched foot. Flip went the burly Bonden, and he and his big pipe lay side by side on the floor.

Ole sent Marie a quick glance. She

returned a frightened look from where she stood over by the fireplace. Then Ole walked away with firm steps singing:

> *Goliath went forth from Gath*
> *For to lay Saul on the mat,*
> *Stamping the rock and tide*
> *With his yard-long stride.*

Ole was quite excited when he came home. "That Bonden-devil will likely go mad some day!" he said as soon as he came in the door. "But I think we have a way out," he added as he went to the cupboard and opened the door. "I have one mark and two shillings in my piggybank and I'm going over to Berg to buy a loaf of bread with the mark and sugar with the shillings. Berg will surely trust me with some coffee, I would think."

"No, don't break your bank to pieces, Ole, a present from Mother when you were only six months old!" his mother protested. He stopped and stood for a long time struggling within himself to make the right decision.

"Yes, the coins shall come out even if it takes hours," he said at last. He took the only table knife in the house and began to fish out first an old half-shilling, then an old worn twelve-shilling piece, and so forth until he had a pile of money on the table amounting to twenty-four shillings. He put the savings bank back in the cupboard with two shillings left in it.

"Do you want me to go, Mother?" he said as he rattled the money in his hand.

"Yes, but it hurts me to see you spend money it has taken nearly fourteen years to save," she answered, the tears rolling down her pale sunken cheeks.

"Oh, don't worry about that, Mother. After New Year's I shall go logging with Tron Snaret every other day, then there will be plenty of money to put in the bank again and some for you, too! Don't cry, Mother!"

He slung the knapsack over his shoulder and ran most of the way to the country store.

He pictured to himself the dark Christmas awaiting them and the road home seemed long and difficult, not only because the four loaves grew heavier but now he thought of his mother's tears and hollow cheeks as she sat with the twins and little Margarete on the floor crying because she was hungry. This distressed him deeply.

At home his mother perceived how discouraged he was, so she asked no unnecessary questions regarding the outcome.

"This will be all of the Christmas fare," he

said, taking the four loaves out of the sack.

"We will get through Christmas Day with this, and then we will get the meal from the mill," his mother replied.

"Yes, we can keep alive, but it appears to me that this life pays meager returns both to you and father when, after a full year of hard and faithful work, day in and day out part of the night too, you are sentenced to bread and water on Christmas Day."

It began to darken and soon Torkil came over the swamp, pulling a load of wood on his ski-sled. He came in, wiped the perspiration from his forehead with his sleeve, and sat down on the bench by the fireplace as little Margarete climbed into his lap. He stroked the hair out of her eyes and patted her cheek, all without saying a word. At last Randi said, "You must be hungry."

"Yes-s, in truth I cannot say otherwise, but the food supply must be running low here."

"That's so, but Ole took twenty-four shillings out of his saving bank and went to the store and bought bread," Randi answered.

This seemed to give Torkil new life. He took off his jacket and hung it on the wall, stirred up the fire, and said to Ole, "Well, if I can get a day off from Bonden this winter, I will go to work in the woods and do some chopping. If Sven Lie will give me the work, I will make enough money to put twenty-four shillings back in the bank again."

Randi took a loaf of bread, cut a slice for Torkil, and was about to cut one more when she looked at Ole , who shook his head. So she put the loaf back in the cupboard. Torkil broke off a bit from his slice and gave it to Margarete. Her sad eyes had followed every motion and saw the bread go back on the shelf. Torkil was not as down-hearted as Randi or his son, for he was happy in the knowledge that there were four whole loaves of bread, a half-barrel of meal at the mill, and lots of water in Sigdal River.

Another pine log on the fire, and the room became bright and cheerful. Randi brought out the spinning wheel after first glancing at a little skein of yarn that hung on the wall -- no, that was too small a Christmas gift for her mother -- and quickly the spinning wheel was whirling. Torkil brought out his pipe, and Ole his book. He read a while but soon put it down. At last Torkel asked, "Bonden evidently was not in good humor today?"

"No, far from it. When I started to explain

and defend myself, he became furious and chased me out of the kitchen. He was so drunk he could barely stand on his feet. I think he should change his ways, for one as inhuman as a wolf can hardly expect happiness and good fortune to come his way."

While father and son sat talking together, the door opened and Guri and Marie entered. "We have come with some food for you from Mother Hovland. Here is a little flour," she said, setting a large pail on the floor. "And here is something to cook," she continued as she took meat, pork, peas, and grits from her apron.

Marie sat down by Ole, took a slate and asked him to write a problem for her. At the same time she put a package of coffee and sugar in his lap. Guri must not see this, for she was too talkative sometimes.

Ole sat down by the fire and wrote for a long time, while Randi heaped thanks and blessings on Guri and Marie and extra thanks to bring home to Gunhild. Then Ole gave the slate to Marie and said, "I have written a problem for you, using letters instead of numbers."

After shaking hands all around and wishing everyone a Merry Christmas, they departed hurriedly for home.

"You were a long time doing your chores tonight, girls! You are making good preparations for Christmas, I can see," Bonden remarked just as soon as they stepped in the house. He was a little shaky on his feet.

The tables in the kitchen and the dining room were laden with food. On the kitchen table were three large bowls of "Risengrynsgrod," a rice porridge, and by the side of each was a huge bowl of milk. In the dining room were four large plates of "Rommegrod," a cream porridge, and on a platter was a rib roast with potatoes, along with a decanter of brandy, a mug of ale, and much more -- silverware, compotes and two large silver candlesticks. Carl Strøm, head clerk in the district judge's office at Lerberg, was Torsten Hovland's only guest, so the table was set for four.

The customary singing before the meal was omitted, for Bonden did not approve of "such nonsense." Later when the brandy began to take effect, Bonden started singing some old drinking songs. Strøm knew a few songs too, and *Pipervigen and Hammesborg* met especially with Bonden's approval.

"You will please excuse me. We have so

much to take care of in the kitchen," Gunhild said at last, appearing to be tired of the concert.

She went out of the dining room with Marie and into the bedroom where Gunhild picked up a hymnbook. She sighed a little, and began in a low voice to read the Christmas story. When she looked up she saw Marie reading something on her slate. Marie did not notice that her mother had walked quietly over to her and, leaning over her shoulder, was reading the poem Ole had written earlier that evening. In it he revealed to Marie that he did not know want and unhappiness when she was near. Her voice was like angels singing, and her face the fairest he had ever seen. He thanked her for all she had given them and prayed God's blessing and guidance on her journey over life's ocean. It was on this night that the shepherds saw the star, as if Marie were the star in his mind that could lead him directly to the manger.

At the end was the note: "Merry Christmas to you and your good Mother is the wish always of your faithful friend, Ole."

*BISMERFUND, a weight measurement that amounts to about twelve pounds.

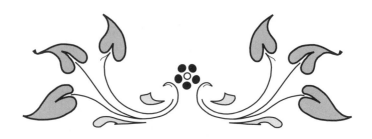

Chapter Seven

The Two Are Confirmed

Again three years have passed. There were elaborate parties at Hovland, and over at Haugen there was the usual perpetual grind and struggle for existence. Ole was up on the saeter in the summer, and in the winter he was in school one day, and at home chopping wood the next. He was not with Marie as much now as when they were small; he went with the boys, and she with the girls.

The time had come when these two should "go to the minister." Ole's parents had in mind having him confirmed the previous year, but Sexton Aas advised them to let him attend school another winter and then he would try to get the farmers to contribute money towards sending Ole to the Seminary. This gave the parents new courage to deny themselves necessities, and accept sacrifice to keep him in school.

The girls and boys met the same day at the rectory. Asle Viig passed by Hovland with his horse and sleigh, so Marie had to ride with him. Her father wanted it that way. So Asle had many advantages over Ole in relation to the minister, something he was not used to at school. It was Asle's privilege to take first place on the bench and Marie had to sit opposite him in the first place for the girls. The cotter's son became number four. It was not long, however, before the minister lost respect for Asle. Seldom did he know his lessons, and he could not answer the questions properly. Ole usually had to answer for him. On the other hand, Marie was far advanced in reading and all the other subjects. She had acquired considerable understanding of religion in school and from books at home that she and her mother studied secretly. She, therefore, earned her place.

When fall came and time for confirmation drew near, there was a tight pinch again for the folks at Haugen. Ole had cut down trees and saved enough to buy homespun cloth for a suit, but where would they find enough money to pay the tailor for making it?

About three weeks before the confirmation Sexton Aas came in at Haugen and asked how things were going with them. Randi was there alone with the little ones, and she told him about the situation from beginning to end.

"I have just now a tailor in the house," said Sexton Aas. "Let Ole come over with the cloth when it is convenient and we will have the suit made. Here is material for a vest from Gunhild Hovland," he continued as he opened a package and took from it a piece of nice black cloth. "Ole is the smartest candidate for confirmation that I have ever sent to the minister in my long experience as a teacher, and he deserves to have nice clothes," the sexton declared.

As soon as Ole came home he was told the wonderful news about the tailor and the vest. The pangs of hunger suddenly left him and he went directly over to Sexton Aas' to be measured.

"You are already a grownup man," said Paul, the tailor, as he took his measurements. "I am twice as old as you, but I would not dare to wrestle with you!"

"I wouldn't wrestle with you either before you get my suit ready, for I might happen to hurt you," Ole jested.

Now the worst was over, but Ole also had to have twenty-four shillings to give to the minister as was the custom when confirmed. To ask for the money from Bonden would be useless, so Ole went to Sven Lie and agreed to chop three cords of birch wood for him at eighteen shillings a cord. Sven selected a piece of woodland for Ole not so far from the Hovland barns.

Early Wednesday morning Ole came carrying his axe in the crook of his arm. He appeared to be very happy, and he had in mind that by nightfall his contract should be fulfilled. His father had agreed to go over to Lie in the evening and collect the fifty-four shillings he had earned, while Ole went over to the sexton to get the new clothes. Ole walked down the path listening to the singing of the birds. The lark sent his trills into the enchanting morning air, and Ole remembered a song he had learned at school:

> Earth glitters with trembling fragrant dew,
> The lark soars into far-off blue,
> The brook flows away with the clouds
> As morning sounds about me crowd.

Before the song was finished he became aware that the singing had become a duet, and as he looked around he saw Marie half-hidden behind the hedge. She came with Guri to the summer barn and motioned Ole over, with her bare arm waving over the hedge. He ran quickly over to her.

"We girls shall be taken over to the minister today," whispered Marie to him. "Watch for me when we go by here. I will lag behind the others a little and drop something on the road for you."

As soon as she had said this she hurried away to join Guri.

Ole began now with increasing energy to chop down the birch trees.

When Marie came back from the barn her father said, "I shall attend a meeting of officers today and you can ride with me over to the minister, but get ready quickly. Here are the two fives I promised you yesterday to give to the minister."

Marie's heart sank at once and she thought her plans had been thwarted, but after saying a few words to her mother she hurried to her room and came back all ready to go.

Together they drove towards the minister's home. Bonden glanced stiffly down at Ole as they drove past him and called scoffingly, "Yes, there you have met your match!"

"Yes, yours also, as far as hardness is concerned," answered Ole, who assumed that Bonden referred to the birch log he was splitting.

While Bonden looked to the other side, where a herd of cattle was grazing, Marie took the opportunity to drop a little package from the back of the buggy.

They had not gone far before they disappeared into the woods, and Ole, with pounding heart, ran out to the road and picked up the package. He was surprised to find two sandwiches in the package and a letter containing a five-dollar coin wrapped in a handkerchief of the finest linen with the letters OTH embroidered in red thread on it. The contents of the letter were as follows:

Dearest friend Ole T. Haugen!
With Mother's approval, I send you here with a five-dollar piece, which is half of the amount Father gave me to give to the minister. We have always shared our joys and sorrows and as I know it would be hard for you or your parents to get money for this purpose, I shall, with the assurance that we neither steal from father nor the minister, divide the money with you. It will reach the intended place just the same. I am glad that

half of the favor that the ten dollars brings is
diverted to you tomorrow and will close with a
sincere greeting from you girl friend,
Marie T. Hovland

This was really too much for Ole. He sat down on a stump and pondered and pondered, but could not conceive any particular wrong in it. However, at the same time that he was touched by Marie's sacrifice to make him happy, he could in his heart not deny that he would rather have been rid of the money and used his own fifty-four shillings to give to the minister instead.

Arriving home he told his mother proudly, "Now the three cords of wood are ready, and good measure it is, too."

"That's good. Father will go by Lie's tonight and get the money."

"Good, but I have received money from another place also," said Ole as he pulled a knotted cloth from his shirt with one hand and scratched behind his ear with the other.

"Where in the world have you gotten so much money, my boy? Is it real?" cried his mother dubiously. She had heard about such coins before but had never seen them.

After Ole had read the letter to her, she

exclaimed, "God bless her! She is kind-hearted! She does not realize how much good she can do for you and all of us, but---."

Ole gave one of the sandwiches to Margarete and divided the other between the four-year-old twins, Per and Guri. Then he ate his dinner; food no doubt of the coarser kind. Then he washed up to go over to the sexton's home.

The clothes were ready now and the sexton asked him to try them on.

He put a black hat on Ole's head and said, "Well, now they are not going to take you for a cotter's son over at the Seminary. Everything fits you very well, and with your natural ability they are more likely to take you for a minister's son!"

Ole now said farewell to the school and his teacher. The few well-chosen words he spoke came from the depths of his heart.

Torkil, who did not know what had happened during the day, came the same evening to Lie and asked for Sven. He was told that Sven had gone to a relative's in Numedal and would not return for several days.

"That is bad," said Torkil sadly. "I was expecting to get the shillings coming to Ole for chopping the wood."

"He probably had all the money with him. I don't think there is a shilling in the house," answered Mother Lie.

"Well then, I have no idea where a poor man can turn. Ole has worked hard to earn these shillings and rejoiced over being able to give them to the minister tomorrow. God knows what the minister will do with a poor empty-handed boy. He could refuse to let him be confirmed and compel him to go another year and suffer shame and loss."

"Yes, that is very bad. However much I regret it there is no way I can think of to help you. But I shall suggest to you that you go by Hovland and speak to Gunhild. Surely, she has so many shillings that she can help you out, and then she can get them back when Sven returns."

Happy as a bird, Torkil went away from Lie. He was as sure that he could get the money as if he had it in his hand. Arriving at Hovland he whispered something in Gunhild's ear, but she only answered, "Ole will very likely get out of the dilemma. Don't you worry!"

This was a let down for Torkil and he went home very downhearted, wondering if Gunhild should have become as hard as

The Cotter's Son

Bonden. His doubts vanished when he returned home.

The following day, on the way to the minister, Asle Viig was rattling silver coins in his pocket, and called over to Ole, "Do you have money for the preacher today, verse-writer?"

"Not much, Mr. Wood-chewer, but you don't expect much from poor people."

"Then you will be placed last in line next Sunday, for the minister likes money," said Asle with visible pride in the thought that he would be at the head of the line.

Ole's attitude became serious and he answered, "I see in the confirmation more than the winning of rank on the church floor. As long as I am not placed outside the church door, I will know I am in God's house, and the vow I take I am sure will be heard."

One by one the confirmands were called in to be catechized. Ole was the fourth to be questioned. As usual, he gave excellent answers to all the questions and the minister praised him almost as much as he did some of the farmer's sons, for his Christian understanding and recital of baptismal pledges. When the minister had finished his short sermon, Ole took his five dollars out of his vest pocket and gave to him. As he turned to go the minister spoke to him, "I am sure that these five dollars have cost you and your parents many drops of perspiration, perhaps nights of sleep and they are proof from you and yours of the love of God's Holy Word and those who spread His message, together with respect for the Holy Act that lies before you. Accept my thanks. To you who are a convert and in whom God has bestowed great gifts, I wish you success from my heart and good luck throughout life, and hope that you will be faithful until the end so to inherit the crown of life, regardless of your rank or ancestry. I will give you the place you deserve, namely the first in line. Now goodbye."

This praise did not have the intended effect on Ole, for even before the minister was through speaking it occurred to him that he had not done the right thing in accepting the money from Marie and receiving good will at Torsten Hovland's expense. But it was too late now. He sought to console himself by the fact that Marie would have received double the blessing if she had given both the fives herself, so it was her loss since she gave it of her own free will and not her father's.

The day of confirmation arrived. It was a beautiful Sunday in September. The air was clear and refreshing. The morning sun cast glory on the already golden woods, and gilded the mountain ash and birch, the ash berries looking like shining red pearls. Everywhere people were seen on their way to church, some driving, others on horseback, but most of them on foot, including Ole and his parents.

When the time came for the confirmands to take their places, Asle hurriedly took the top place, but then Ole came forward with confident steps past the whole line and stood in front of him. He glanced quickly over to Marie, who blushed and again resumed her sober devotional attitude. Everyone looked in wonderment and many were not sure if it was the cotter's son, while both Torsten Hovland and Thore Viig sat envied him from the bottom of their hearts.

The years between baptism and confirmation had made so many changes. Now the two stood facing each other, she beautiful and innocent as a lily; he bold and gallant, nearly a full-grown man in whose face was an expression of seriousness, determination, and mildness. All who saw them had to acknowledge that they had never seen a nicer group of confirmands in Holum Church.

The minister gave a long and impressive sermon for the young people and their parents. His theme was that "The Lord's ways are not our ways and in whatever paths He leads His people He has in His wisdom plans that are for the good of those who love Him."

During the catechization, Ole made clear his religious understanding and impressed the congregation with his great gift for speaking. After the services there were many comments about him from both rich and poor.

The Haugen folds found an opportunity to talk with Sexton Aas and thank him for his goodness to Ole from first to last. Sexton Aas then told them he had been asked over to Hovland for dinner and that he intended to come over to Haugen in the afternoon, which pleased parents and son.

One wagon after another joined Marie Hovland's party while Ole's gathering was few in number, just as it was after his baptism. There were only his parents and himself, and their hearts were as full of happiness as any others could be.

After the Haugen folks had finished their

meager fare, Torkil said, "Now I think Sexton Aas is coming! Put on the coffeepot! He surely has not had any coffee at Hovland yet!"

"But dear me Torkil! I have only one coffee cup. Run over to Svartbraaten as fast as you can and borrow a pair of cups. The sexton surely cannot sit and drink coffee alone."

Before Randi finished saying this, Torkil dashed out the back door and stumbled over the little pig that was eating its midday meal. It squealed so vigorously that it was heard way over to Hovland.

"The cotter folk over at Haugen must be butchering their little pig so they can have something to treat the sexton," the party quipped among themselves.

The sexton on his way to Haugen could not but wonder, too.

Sexton Aas stayed at Haugen until late in the evening and talked with them about how they would provide money for Ole, and it was decided that as soon as winter came he should go to the Asker Seminary.

Chapter Eight

The Cotter's Boy
Is Charged With Stealing

That very week, Sexton Aas took a list of the wealthier people in the neighborhood and solicited contributions. He placed his own name on top of the list for a contribution of two dollars.

Nearly all were willing to give money to such a worthy cause, for not only was Ole well liked but his ability was also highly regarded. The donors were of the opinion that the money would come back to them with good interest. They were certain he would make a good teacher who could replace Sexton Aas, soon to retire. The gifts were recorded on the list with the understanding that when a sufficient amount was subscribed, Ole would take the list himself and go to the givers and receive the money personally, thanking each one. Torsten Hovland and Thore Viig were the only ones who refused to give. Within a few days the pledged sum was greater than expected and it was sufficient for two years at the teacher's college.

On the Sunday following confirmation there was communion at Holum Church. After the service the minister invited the Hovland family to dinner. Torsten was a commune counsellor and had some papers that required the signature of the minister. Inasmuch as he did not have any qualms about doing it on a Sunday, the minister did not hesitate and they took leave of the ladies to enter the private office of the minister. As he was looking over the papers, Torsten noticed a list of names, and as it appeared familiar he became curious and pulled his chair closer. He clearly read the names:

> Marie T. Hovland - - - - Five dollars
> Sigrid H. Stensrud - -- - Three dollars
> Astrid T. Berg - - - - - - Four dollars
> Karen P. Moe - - - - - Three dollars

Further down the boy's names were listed as:

> Asle T. Viig - - - - - - Four dollars

Nils T. Moe - - - - - - Three dollars
Soren P. Braaten - - - Sixty dollars
Ole T. Haugen - - - - - Five dollars

That was enough for Torsten, who well knew that this was the list of contributions by the confirmands and at once he burst out saying, "Here I discover a fraud! And I shall certainly help that fellow to enter prison, instead of the teacher's college he is trying to get into."

The minister did not understand what he was referring to, and became red in the face. He bent over Bonden and said, "May I ask in what does this fraud consist?"

"I sent ten dollars with my daughter as a little recognition to the minister the day the confirmands were examined for confirmation and if I now am not mistaken in what I see on this paper, our cotter's boy, who has been so highly praised for his wisdom as well as for his honesty, has been at his tricks and has filched five dollars from my little girl, so she gave only half of the money--enough for a sexton but not for an honored minister."

"Oh, it is a liberal offering anyway. I owe you many thanks!" said the minister.

"Yes, but then this wretch, who could not produce twelve shillings honestly, advanced himself to the top of the list and became the first one on the church floor -- all at my expense. He should be punished!"

Bonden's voice had now become so high-pitched that it was heard in the next room and cut like a knife into Marie's heart. Her mother, too, sat stunned.

The minister was shocked at the information about how the cotter's son had obtained his elevation. "I regret," he said, "that this has happened in my congregation, and especially among my confirmands. I agreed to sign a recommendation for Ole Haugen for enrollment in the Teacher's College inasmuch as this boy has great gifts that should be used, but this seems to be a well-founded reason for retracting my promise, for I cannot now attest to his good morals or spotless deportment."

"No, I believe that both the boy and society as a whole would fare better if he had only half of his gifts," Bonden mumbled to himself. "For now we see to what purpose he uses them."

As these events were taking place in the minister's home the Haugen folks sat with their son at Sexton Aas'. They had gone home with him and enjoyed a good dinner.

The sexton brought out a large sheet of paper from his cabinet and gave it to Ole.

"With this list in your pocket you can claim your net worth to be exactly one hundred thirty-three dollars and sixty shillings. I believe you are the only cotter's son in the whole valley worth so much at your age. All you have to do is to call on those who have signed here, and you will find that the money is there ready for you. We believe that this will take you through two years in the Teacher's College, and I have no doubt that you can master the examinations with a first-class record. Then you can come back and assume the duties of teaching, relieving me, for I am old and need rest."

Parents and son thanked the old teacher heartily and said that they could never pay him for all the goodness he had shown them. They left the sexton's home in the best of spirits and talked on the way home about their wonderful sexton who will take poor people into his house and even treat them to food and drink. The Haugen folks had never experienced anything like this in their lives. There had been enough of clouds, and just a little sunshine, on their horizon. It was decided that the very next morning Ole should start out with his list.

The next morning came and Ole dressed himself in his confirmation suit. The birds twittered upon the sod roof of the cottage and inspired Ole to sing about Him Who knew every fish in the ocean. It was as if the tune was a prayer that God also would listen and look upon those in the cottage, even though small and lowly. He felt that he owed thanks for all the good things that had fallen in his lap. They were not earned. It was as if a higher power stood by his side all the time; gave him good, kind parents, brothers, and sisters, and more than that, one that he . . .

He was suddenly interrupted in his thoughts as the door opened and Torsten Hovland and Sheriff Bye stepped in.

"We are here to take you to the 'Teacher's College'," Torsten said in a taunting manner. "I know that you have not collected any of your beggar's list yet, so now I will go bail for you." He turned to Sheriff Bye, pointed at Ole and said, "There is the culprit!"

Ole's mother now grasped the situation, and became even paler than before. Suddenly she lost consciousness and dropped to the floor, hitting her head against the fireplace. Blood flowed from the cut on her forehead and the small children, still clutching her dress, trembled beside her and tried to awaken their mother.

"I will not go with you before my mother gains consciousness," Ole declared. "Then you may take me as far as law and justice will permit you." Ole spoke in a manner that touched the sheriff, but the half-drunk Bonden showed no sympathy.

Ole laid his mother on the bed and said a few comforting words to the bewildered children. He forced water into her mouth and washed the cut. Soon there were signs of life.

"Give her some whiskey and she will soon liven up!" said Bonden, and drew a bottle from his pocket.

"Keep yourself away from her!" said Ole angrily. "The whiskey you need yourself. I will not stand for anyone making a fool of my mother. She is too honest and good for that, even if she is poor. I am not afraid to speak my mind in the presence of the sheriff, though it should be the last day to enjoy my liberty. She lies there pale and thin, in shabby clothes on a hard bed, and yet she is a far better human being than you standing there, you who brags about being the richest man in the valley. But remember, the day may well come when you will have to give an account for your imagined wealth."

"He has gone crazy!" said Bonden to the sheriff, who for the first time saw and heard the cotter's son and thought just the opposite.

"Bring my father home and I will go with you," said Ole.

"No, I have authority over him," Bonden answered.

"Yes, that may be so," said the sheriff, "But the woman is sick, so I cannot take him away before there is someone here to take care of her."

Torkil, who was working in the fields over at Hovland, was brought home immediately. Now his dreams for his son in the Teacher's College were shattered.

Ole said some cheering words to his parents, gave little Margarete the fifty-four shillings which Sven Lie paid the previous Saturday, and asked her to go to Berg's and buy bread with them. The three drove over to the sheriff's office. Ole was placed under lock and key to await the outcome of the trial to be held in extra session at Lerberg the following October fifteenth.

As they drove away from Haugen, someone was standing at a window looking after Ole, just as she had done when he, as a boy, went off to herd cattle. Both handkerchief and window frame were wet with tears, but that was something no one ever saw or found out.

Ole was not worried about the final outcome during the time he was imprisoned, but the thought of his parents, crushed under the sorrow of his absence, weighed heavily on his mind. He realized that they thought the case was much more serious than the actual facts would prove. Furthermore it was painful to think how it would hurt Marie, who would suffer with him.

The day of the trial arrived and Ole was brought to court and charged with cheating and appropriating money for himself from Torsten Hovland's money; for which, according to the district judge's reading of the criminal law, paragraph twenty-six, he could be sentenced to six months imprisonment, if there were no counterproof.

"I admit none of the counts stated in the charge," Ole answered in a clear and calm voice. "They are as false as the one who has made the charge against me. I will ask that Marie Hovland be permitted to explain the situation, inasmuch as her statements will more likely be accepted as fact than mine."

Bonden went into the waiting room and brought back Marie, expecting damaging testimony from her. He had spent the last few days in giving her instructions as to what to say when questioned, and did not expect her to dare say anything else.

Marie had no sooner come into the courtroom than she glanced over to Ole, who was restraining a choking throat. It was plain to see that she had neither slept nor eaten much since the last time they had met, and her hair hung in disarray on her pale cheeks.

When asked how Ole had connived to get the money from her, she replied, "Ole has never lured anything from me, either money or anything else. He is too honest for that. If there is to be any punishment, for God's sake take me and send him home to his parents. I threw a package down on the road for him the day I drove with father over to the minister's house, and he was completely ignorant of the contents of the package, or any money in it, until he had opened it. I will admit that it may seem to have been the wrong thing to do, but I have the confident hope that God, Who planted love in my heart, never would have permitted the plan to have come to completion if it were a sin."

"The money was given to me. I was the owner of it before I gave any away. The money was intended for the minister, and to him it did go. The money was not sent to the minister to pay a debt that father owed. It was a gift. When Ole was accused of bringing only half of the present to the one it was intended for, why did not Father accuse him or at least reprimand him for the many times he received half of the bread which Father asked me to give to the dog? The dog took Ole for the giver, and in his own way thanked him and was friendly, making Ole and me very happy. If the minister puts such great importance on money that he promotes or sanctifies anyone in his sacred charge for the sake of a gift, then he will have a harder time to clear himself on the last day than both Ole and I."

The explanation she gave, sealed with tears, made a great impression on the authorities. All was quiet a while. At last the eighth district judge broke the spell and said, "I do not find any punishable guilt in this case. The defendant, Ole Torkilsen Haugen, is declared free of any guilt!"

It was as if rays of sunshine passed over Marie's face. Without being noticed, Marie smiled to Ole and disappeared through the door.

Chapter Nine

Bonden Sinks Deeper And Deeper

While Bonden did not succeed in getting Ole imprisoned, he nevertheless was the cause of preventing him from entering the Teacher's College. The money subscribed by the farmers was designated for Ole, but when the minister refused to attest the document, it became void and the cotter's son was no longer the owner of one hundred and thirty-three dollars and sixty shillings.

Ole did not greatly regret this turn of events. The work of teachers was too meagerly paid, and the time he spent at school could not be used to help his parents.

The morning after, when Torkil had gone to work, Randi and her son were sitting at the breakfast table. "Last night," said Ole, "I decided on a more promising plan than going to the Teacher's College. I hope it will result in a better life for both you and me. The way things are now, the future is dark for all of us. You and Father will both lose your health here working on this farm, and when you get old and cannot work you are on the way to the poor house. That must not happen. Even if I am only a cotter's boy, I shall, if God grants me health, be in America next year, where I do not have to stand with my cap in hand and beg for my money. Even if I have to work hard, in one day over there I could earn more than two weeks here. With some luck I believe it would be possible to release you from this slavery."

"That may be so," sighed his mother, "but for you to go to America means separation as certain as if we followed you to the grave."

"Oh no, don't say that mother! There are many who go to America and return again. Anyway, all will rest in the hands of God."

"But where will you get the money for travel?"

"I shall go out and earn it. I have heard that Sven Lie needs a boy and I am going over there today."

As said, so done. Stopping at the barn, he got his father's consent to the plan. His father also handed him a letter which he recognized as coming from Marie, but not wishing to read it just then he continued on his way to Lie, until he came to the summer barns where he sat down by the wayside, opened the letter, and began to read. It was poetry, surely written during the night.

In the poem Marie told him that she thought of him wherever she was, at home as well as in the woods and meadows, forgetting everything else. In her sleep she saw him before her. She never went to bed without taking a glimpse at the cottage and listening for his quick walk, or the sound of his voice as he talked or sang.

When she knelt beside him in the church, she wrote, she had thought so intensely about him that God was all but crowded out of her mind. Now she saw everything turn to grief, and she herself was responsible for the loss of happiness for both. She well deserved punishment, but why must it strike him also? She had literally sent him to prison and wrecked his plans to go to college. For that she could only expect that he would be done with her, even wholly banish her from his mind. She begged him not to. She would think of him to the very end of life. Even if their happiness were destroyed, she was sure of one thing, that her intentions were good.

Ole put the letter in his pocket and continued on his way, his face thoughtful and his eyes red and swollen.

The folks at Lie were very fond of him and he soon reached an agreement with Sven for a year of service. He would receive twenty-two dollars in cash. Ole began working the same week, and both Ole and Sven found the arrangement satisfactory. Ole was soon his own self again.

He seldom went to dances or sought the company of the young people of the parish. Rather, he used idle moments for reading or writing. He was not a little poetically gifted, and for his age wrote many good poems, inspired by his wandering and work in the woods, and the solitude of the saeter. His few close friends now were the folks at Lie and Sexton Aas, and he went to visit his parents every Sunday. Whenever he saw people other than these, he often heard uncomplimentary remarks regarding the Teacher's College or being a "jailbird," but that was something that did not bother him much.

Long before the year was over, Ole and Sven had agreed to continue their work agreement another year. This time he should receive thirty dollars and in addition be supplied with all the necessary clothing. That was good pay for the time, and most of it he gave to his parents. With the ten dollars he saved and the thirty dollars he would get for the coming year, he believed he could go to America.

Marie was seventeen years old the following spring, and she had many admirers among the valley's best matrimonial prospects -- something not to wonder at, for she was the most beautiful girl in the valley and the only child to inherit the large family farm. But it was well known that it was useless to propose to her. Bonden was proud of her many suitors, but he made it clear that he wanted Asle Viig to have her. Such had been his intention for a long time. It would be a shame to prevent such a union, and a pity for the girl, he would say, for Asle was such an important young man. Now and then Asle came over to Hovland and Bonden always received him most cordially, but Gunhild and Marie were very busy elsewhere during his visits.

Ole had many secret trysts with Marie that summer. There was so much he wanted her to know, and he assured her more good than bad had come from her part in his arrest and imprisonment, for he believed it was God's plan for another and better life for him than teaching would have been. He assured her that he was just as fond of her now as before, and he would always think of her as long as he lived, just as she had avowed in her poems to him. When he told her of his plans to go to America, she at first despaired over them, but as they talked together she gathered confidence and relied on Ole's strength and determination for a happy outcome.

Towards fall she wrote a letter to Ole which she secretly sent to him, confiding that she had something on her heart she wanted to talk with him about, asking him to meet her in the garden next Saturday night. She added that it would be wonderful to be with him again at the very place where they played together in those happy carefree days. Should something prevent her from coming, he must forgive her and leave a note under the big stone so she would know he had received the letter and had been there.

After everyone had gone to bed at Lie, Ole removed his work clothes, dressed in his best, and took a fine white handkerchief out of his trunk. By the light of the fire he wrote the letters MTH on a piece of paper and put it in his pocket with the handkerchief. He walked over to Hovland in a lighter and happier mood than ever before. He felt as if he were in a dream, and with great anticipation set out for the trysting place with its many happy reminders of their childhood days. Arriving there shortly, he climbed the fence and hid behind the bushes in such a way that he could look up to the window of Marie's room. A light was burning there and through the curtains he could see Marie moving about. He sat a long time looking towards the window, and finally he thought he heard light footsteps on the stairs. "Now she is coming!" he thought, and turned and looked toward the path. No, he had fooled himself, she was not coming. Time passed and he became uncertain whether she would come at all. Then he took the paper he had brought out of his pocket, placed it on a flat stone, and by the light of the moon he wrote:

The moon is shining, stars are twinkling, could you only see I am waiting. Then I know you would come down the stairs to me. But you cannot. Not yet, it seems. Still I hope that you will risk it when all are sleeping.

I am sitting here thinking about the days when we were little. We played here with no one to interfere, and those days live in my mind as the dearest of memories. Now we must be so secretive and quiet, and however much I want to go to you and see you, I dare not. But you must always remember one thing, that when the right time comes we shall surely be together. It may be a long wait, but it will. Then I shall be yours, and you mine.

I look up to your window as I have been doing all evening, and imagine that now you are resting on your pillow. Shall I really have to go away from here without having seen you and talked with you? If I had wings, I would fly to your window.

Then good night to you! Dream about me! I shall go home now and be sleeping soon, dreaming of you. Then we can meet in our dreams and love will enter and grow in our hearts, yours and mine.

He folded the paper in the handkerchief, hid both under the stone, and leisurely went back to Lie. In his imagination he was soaring up to her room to carry her away. Her father and Asle were shooting arrows after them up in the air. One hit Marie and wounded her, but the wound was healed when he gently touched it.

When fall came and Ole's year of service was at an end, he had enough money to buy passage to America on a sailing vessel, but not enough for the steamship ticket to Chicago, so he stayed on with Lie that winter also. He was determined to leave early in the spring on a sailing vessel, for none such left in the fall.

Christmas night he asked for and was given a leave so he could be home with his parents a few days. On his way he stopped at Berg to buy a few things to cheer his parents. They were glad to have him at home with them, but they could not banish from their minds the thought that this might be the last Christmas they would be together -- a probability that put a damper on the happiness and good cheer in the cottage. The table was set and presented a slightly richer appearance than normally. When all were seated Torkil brought out the hymn book, and Ole struggled to hold back his tears as he looked at his parents, the twins, and sister Margarete, and thought of leaving them. As they were about to start singing the door opened and Marie entered. "We are having such an unpleasant Christmas Eve at home that I wanted to come over here for awhile," she said, as sobs choked her voice.

She sat down beside Ole and he took her hand in his.

"Father came home drunk around dinner time, with Asle Viig and Carl Strøm," Marie told them. "They have been drinking all evening, so Mother and I sat by ourselves. Asle wanted to talk to me, and father urged him on. But I have never been able to stand him, from the first time I saw him, and I kept away for a long time by hiding in a wardrobe. Then when it became quiet downstairs Mother came up and told me that everyone had gone to sleep, so I could go down. But just as I reached the bottom step Asle sprang out of the darkness and without a word roughly pulled me towards him. I cried out, and Erick came and set me free. Father, who was sleeping on the sofa, jumped up and came towards me, and steadying himself on tables and chairs, he began to scold me, saying "You are a 'fraid-rabbit' and a dumb-bell!" The sight of my father and the thought of the way Christmas was being profaned . . . poor Mother! She has so little strength, and must put up with so much that

I often find her crying. If Father does not stop such a life, he will bring Mother to an early grave!"

"Hush, there is someone rustling about outside the house," Torkil warned. "Did you put the calf in, Randi?" At that moment the door flew open and Asle Viig staggered in.

"Is my g-girl here?" he stammered.

"I don't know if I am acquainted with your girl," answered Ole. "There are no others here than those you see now."

"Oh y-yes, there I see my gold, - hic - come n-now and - hic - follow me to Viig and taste - hic - our Christmas pudding, Y-you are not so foolish - hic - that you will sit here with the co-cotter's son now that you are a grown girl and have a - hic - little sense. My horse Sleipner* is here and you shall have a - hic - lively ride Come now! Forget about this co-cotter's boy."

"I would rather die in his arms than join you in all your glorious things," said Marie, throwing herself in Ole's arms and crying out, "Protect me from him!"

"Yes, don't be afraid," said Ole "I shall soon tie up that calf."

"You call me a calf! You, the jailbird!" cried Asle, and with fists clenched he approached the bench where Ole was sitting with Marie, "If you don't quit sitting with my girl - hic - I shall quickly teach you that I am no calf but a grown-up - - -"

"Ox!" interrupted Ole. He placed himself between Marie and Asle. "Enough of your nonsense! If you have no other errand here, you had better try to find the same way out as you came in -- the sooner the better for you. This whole afternoon you have been carousing at Hovland and disturbing the Christmas peace there. Then you come here thinking you can carry on the same way; but remember that as long as the cotter's son is here you shall surely not carry on as you please. Furthermore, it looks as if alcohol has robbed you of both your voice and your strength. If you don't take yourself out of here now I shall quickly test your courage too!"

"The man who can throw me out doesn't exist!" Asle shouted. He clenched his fists, gnashed his teeth, and stomped on the floor until the walls rattled in the little cottage and the bottle with the Christmas light tumbled over, leaving the room in darkness. Asle reeled forward and put his hands on Marie, but the next thing he could remember was being thrown out and rolling far down the hillside.

The candle was lighted again and Margarete and the twins crawled from under the bed. Torkil was chewing so hard on his tobacco that the juice ran down his whiskers. Ole, cool as before, tried to quiet Marie and his mother. With some success soon they were singing *In This Sweet Christmas Time*. But Marie could not join them. She sat and cried.

After they had eaten their Christmas supper, Ole accompanied Marie over to Hovland, where he remained outside while she went in to find out how matters stood. Both she and her mother came outside and said that they had not seen Asle since he left the place earlier in the evening, so he must have gone home. Bonden was sleeping on the sofa and Strøm was snoring under the table.

"Stay here tonight," said Gunhild, "We dare not go to bed anyway."

It was a pleasant duty for Ole to have the opportunity to do something for the good Gunhild, who had done so much for him. They went carefully up the stairs and into Marie's room and sat down.

They talked about many things for there

were strong bonds between the three.
Gunhild found the slate which Ole had written on and asked him to write something on
it to Torsten about drinking. Ole declined
and said he thought that would make things
worse. But before he left he had written
something on paper and given it to her saying that she was to give this to Torsten when
the occasion seemed right.

When it was nearly daybreak Guri brought
food up to them. It was not yet daylight
when Ole, as quietly as possible, went down
the stairs to the main entrance. He could not
go through the kitchen, for the servants
would see him. Bonden noticed that someone
came out from Marie's room and down the
stairs. He opened the parlor door and tried to
rub the sleep out of his red eyes and whispered, "Is it you, Asle?"

Ole could see only the shadow-like shape
of the heavy body of Bonden, in the dim
light from the parlor window. He whispered
back, "Yes."

"Did you get a good agreement from the
girl?"

"Yes, very good, my man," Ole tried to talk
like Asle.

"But are you leaving so soon?"

"I don't want anybody to see me, you understand."

"Don't be silly, boy. Everyone knows you shall have her."

"But it is so difficult at first. I would rather go now."

"Sure, but come in and have some brandy."

"Yes, thank you, I will."

"Skaal! Son-in-law!"

"Skaal! Father-in-law!"

"Luck with the girl!"

"Thank you!"

"It is almost a year since I bought this watch for you, the best that was to be found at Watchmaker Olsen's in Drammen. I did not want to give it to you before you and the girl were really engaged. Now I understand you have her consent and I am glad the matter is settled. Here is the watch, your name is engraved on the case."

"Well thank you, but this is too much. I would rather come back tonight and receive it when Marie and Mother Gunhild can be with us."

"You had better take it at once, Asle, or I may take both the watch and the girl before you come back again," said a voice from under the table.

The Cotter's Son

"So you are beginning to limber up,"
Bonden laughed and turned to face the table.
"I did not think we would disturb you. We
have whispered all this time. No, my dear
Strøm, now the girl is sold. Well, sold she is
not. I am not so poor as that, not so poor
that I need to sell either the woman or the
girl. Should I need a couple of thousand, all I
need to do is to write on a piece of paper.
But she is given away to a good man, and to
the one whom she herself likes. You neglect-
ed a good chance last night, my good Strøm.
You bragged about how to get the girl, and
then you went to sleep under the table, away
from it all, and Asle came and put one over
on you. Ha - ha - ha!"

"So this is the way you treat folks at your
Christmas party -- you stand before them,
deliver long sermons, and have them as butts
for your jokes," raved Strøm. He raised himself so quickly that he bumped his head
against the table and shook the glasses on
top.

"You are as crabby as an old woman and
cannot stand a joke," laughed Bonden. "But
you shall have a refresher and drink to the
health of my son-in-law, if you will propose a
toast to him."

"I have no time for either you or Asle," growled Strøm as he emptied the glass.

"But don't you want to drink a toast to Asle?" asked Bonden, raising his glass.

"Yes, certainly," said Strom, who thirsted for another drink.

"I don't want more drink, for I know Marie doesn't like it," answered Ole.

"So you are already under the lash!" taunted Carl. "I shall not begrudge you the union. No, the girl that shall be mine will certainly have to put up with my taking a dram. I will not trade my drinking for any girl. Father drank, his father drank, and I would like to see the men who could compare with them in strength and heart. Yes, drink we shall as long as we live. Skaal, Torsten!"

"I agree with you, and I have my own ideas about Asle and his sobriety in the long run," Bonden added, and finished his dram. He took Ole by the hand and said, "I like to see you try to please the girl in everything reasonable, but take a few drinks as before. It harms no one. But since you have become so bashful since you were up with the girl, I will not keep you any longer. Do as you said, and come back tonight. You have rough working hands, Asle! Why do you do so much rough work, you can afford to take it easy? I shall see your father about that."

Happy as a freed bird, Ole slipped out through the door. The sun had just come up, but heavy curtains shut out the light in the parlor. Gunhild and Marie had stood at the top of the steps and listened intently. They wondered at their parting words, when Ole thanked Bonden for everything, and Bonden had replied that it was nothing. He could easily have recognized his strange guest had he been sober and clear-eyed.

Asle, of course, did not come to Hovland on the evening of Christmas Day. When Strøm had gone home after imbibing many more drinks and singing a few Christmas hymns about "Bryggesjaueren" and "Vaterlandsenken" and the like, Bonden went in, wished them a merry Christmas, and seated himself on the sofa. After some time he asked, "Isn't Asle home tonight?"

"Yes he is, but he does not feel well."

"That's too bad! But he was well when he left us today."

"Today? No, now you must be dreaming, my dear Torsten. The boy came home late last night and since then he has not been out of his bed."

"What are you saying, Thore? Did the boy come home last night? That cannot be possible! I have never believed in ghosts before, but certainly things begin to look queer. Is he very sick? Maybe he is destined to die and this is an omen."

"He says he has a headache, and it is probably very bad too -- he has bruises all over his body," answered Thore Viig as he brought drinks from the corner cupboard. Placing them on the table, he added, "Have a drink, and we shall go up to him after a while."

"All right, skaal! It would be a pity if the boy should lie down and die. I hoped we could marry the children, and in that way become related. They have had so much in common all the time, these young folks. They were schoolmates, were confirmed on the same day, and had God knows how many other mutual interests. All the while they have thought so much of each other, and 'when children have their own way they don't cry,' says the proverb."

"Surely we would never object, but let us go up and see him."

The two went up to Asle's room. Bonden entered and greeted him: "Good evening, son-in-law! You are not so well? And how pale you are! What has happened to you?"

"I can tell you everything," sighed Asle. "Last night after we had been drinking a little together, as you know, I found out that Marie had gone over to Haugen."

"Haugen! What are you saying boy? Was Marie over to Haugen last night?"

"Yes, and I went over there to ask her in a nice way to come home with me. I tied the horse among the pines below the hill and entered the cottage quietly and courteously. But the haughty 'teacher,' the poet, the jailbird, your cotter's son, became mouthy and used language not fit for decent people. I am no more than human, but I had little in my top, so I just asked him to keep still, for I had something to talk to Marie about. I didn't know that anything was wrong. But instantly he put out the light, sprang at me, and lifted me up so my head hit the round logs in the ceiling. When I awoke I was lying face down in the gravel halfway down the hill. Ole has never been a man to give me a licking, and he never will be. The devil himself is helping the people on the hill, I'll bet my horse and sleigh on that."

Torsten Hovland did not understand all that Asle was saying, but sat and mumbled something to himself. When Asle had finished he said more to himself than those around him, "If only that scoundrel had taken the watch with him he should have had his free housing during the winter."

After that he did not mention the ghost he had seen Christmas morning.

While Asle was telling his story, the cotter's son was sitting with Marie and her mother at Hovland. He told them about the hearty reception Bonden had given him before he managed to leave. Mother Hovland smiled -- something she had not done for years.

* THOR, the slayer of evil spirits, the mythical second principal god of ancient Scandinavians whose horse was supposed to be of that name.

* SLEIPNER was also the 350-ton schooner-brig which pioneered direct contact by ship between Norway and Chicago and opened the St. Lawrence Deep Sea Waterway for direct trade between Europe and the Middle West. The dauntless little vessel carried both passenger and freight and its arrival in Chicago on August 2, 1862, attracted wide-

spread attention. It later made three similar voyages in 1863, 1864, and 1865. It was lost at sea in 1870 in the Mediterranean. In observance of the centennial of the arrival of the ship, after a long preparation, a plaque was erected in Chicago in the summer of 1962.

Chapter Ten

The Two Bid
Each Other Goodbye

"I wonder if it is the Lord's will that I shall listen to you again, or is this the last time?" Ole mused as he heard the cuckoo over in the meadows the following spring. And as he saw one flower after another pushing up between the stones around the cottage he felt himself sink lower in spirit. It was as if it were preordained that his journey must be delayed until now when springtime awakened all nature from winter's sleep to bid him goodbye.

He had the ticket in his pocket, knapsack on his back, and his trunk was already on the wheelbarrow outside the door. The family gathered inside the hut. Few words were spoken, but there were many tears. Little

Margarete smiled when she looked at the silk handkerchief she held in her hand, but cried when she looked at her brother, ready to leave. The twins, Per and Guri, each had a picture book they were busy with; but even they cried, without knowing the reason why.

Quickly Ole tore himself away from his mother and without further words he went to the door. He looked at his mother and pointed to a large book which lay on the table. Torkil followed his son outside, grabbed the handles of the wheelbarrow, and started downhill. Ole followed him slowly, and when they had reached the Hovland farmhouse he said to his father, "Go slowly ahead, I must step in here and say goodbye."

This time Bonden took more kindly to him than he had before, probably because he was glad to be rid of him for many reasons. He asked Ole to come into the house, offered him a drink, which Ole declined with thanks, and wished Ole a good trip.

Ole kept his courage as long as possible and spoke clearly and cheerfully until he faced Gunhild. Then he broke into tears. She tucked a piece of paper money in his hand as she said farewell and could only say to him, "God be with both of you."

He did not see Marie and thought the reason might be that she dared not trust herself and was afraid to come downstairs. He took a few steps up, then turned and went out through the kitchen. "When a person can't, then he can't," he thought.

Ole walked with rapid strides down the road to catch up with his father, who would need his help over the Lie hill. He regretted so much that he could not see Marie and say goodbye to her -- then a whisper came from the rosebushes.

"Ole, will you come here?"

He looked around, put the knapsack down by the fence and jumped over it. Both sat down on the big stone in the garden and embraced each other. For a long while they did not say a word. Then at last Marie broke the silence. Taking the handkerchief with the initials on it from her bosom she dried her eyes and said, "I am happy at least that we can part on this precious place. Since fate has arranged that we shall not be together for a time, now both my first and last memories will linger here. I cannot recall any dearer memory than playing with you in the shade of these rosebushes that have grown up with us. Now I see you here for the last -- if it should be God's will that you never -- yes, one thing you can feel certain about. Ole, wherever you go . . ."

Emotion choked her, and Ole said, "Three things we must never let go of, Marie -- Hope, Faith, and Love. We'll cast anchor here and keep steadfast hope that here we shall meet again in three years. For my parent's sake, and for your and my own sake, I shall work to the last ounce of energy to get ahead so that your fortune shall not depend on Asle's wealth. Then maybe we will get your father's consent. If not, we can with good conscience belong to each other, assured that it is His will, Who is Father of all. Have faith in Him and in me. Then nothing can take you away from me, my darling, remember this:

God's will prevails, I cannot stray.
In heaven will be our wedding day.

After a moment of silence, a handclasp, a kiss, Ole swung the knapsack on his back again. He walked a few steps and took out his handkerchief with the red initials on it, turned and waved it repeatedly until his eyes could no longer distinguish her figure, the loveliest rose in the garden.

Torkil was resting midway up the long steep Lie hill when Ole caught up with him. Ahead of them lay a long and laborious road -- forty-nine miles to Drammen -- over which they must push their wheelbarrow. Ole sat down with Torkil and took out the paper Gunhild had given him and he read:

Our dear Ole!

> *This will probably be the last time that we shall see each other here below, as I have a pre-monition that I shall not be very old. I have there-fore this prayer for you, that whatever you do, never let her go whose happiness lies only with you. I shudder at the thought that she might be left motherless, yes, I might well say fatherless also, and be without you. You must, for her sake and mine, take courage, for regardless of position or heritage you are a much better man than either Asle or Carl Strøm, and far dearer to her than any prince. God grant that your will cannot be shaken and that you may return at the time you decide. Risk all to attain your goal.*

> *A good journey is wished you by the one who loves you as a mother.*

> *Gunhild Hovland*

After two days of grueling effort they reached Drammen. The emigrant ship was due to leave in about two days. To husband his meager savings, Ole went aboard ship and his father was permitted to spend the night with him.

The next morning was difficult for Ole as he stood on the deck and sadly watched his father trudge up Strømso Street with his wheelbarrow.

The journey across was long and stormy. On June the seventeenth, Ole stepped on land on the other side of the ocean, in the city of Quebec, where he immediately wrote to his parents and Marie. He continued by steamboat to his destination, Chicago, and arrived there after considerable difficulty on the last day of June.

Chapter Eleven

Bitter Disappointments

Captain Hansen accompanied the immigrants to Chicago and did everything to help the newcomers. He went with Ole up to the employment office where, after paying his last two dollars, he was given a ticket that would take him to the small town of Carlton, Illinois. Here he was to work on a railroad bridge for two dollars per day plus three and a half dollars a month for board and bed. "Thirty-seven dollars a month in my pocket," Ole mused. "Surely, now I am in America. But what shall my poor father think when he hears of this, for he receives only eight shillings."

On his arrival at Carlton he found no Norsemen, nearly all were Irish. The work was hard for him in the beginning, but as he became accustomed to it he became one of the best workmen, and got the reputation among the Irish of being a smart newcomer. His fellow laborers could not resist mocking his Scandinavian accent when he tried to speak English. This became an annoyance, and only after thrashing a couple of men very neatly did it stop, and he was accepted among them.

Ole quickly learned to understand and speak some English and he was happy in his new environment, dreaming night and day about the future. He had worked two weeks and his greatest desire was to write home, but how could he manage it with only three cents in his pocket. He was not promised money before the work was finished the last of September. He had heard the contractor tell his fellow workingmen that he had no money to give a merchant named Davis in Carlton.

One day Ole discovered that a Norseman was employed at a warehouse in Carlton, and after work the next Saturday night he went over there and to his joy met Nils Wang, who gave him a friendly welcome and seemed pleased to meet one of his country-men. Nils was about twenty-seven years old and had a mild and easy manner. Even if he was now engaged in rough manual labor, one could detect that he had seen better days.

Ole told him about his home, and Wang listened with much interest. At last Ole said, "I would like so much to write home but I have no money for paper and postage."

Wang took a half-dollar from his pocket and gave it to him with the remark, "Is this enough?"

"Yes, more than enough," answered Ole as he explained his working conditions and told him when he could pay back the fifty cents.

"There is no hurry about it. I get money whenever I ask for it, but not more than from hand to mouth. Do you want a dram or something else?"

"No thanks, I don't drink."

"I like to hear that. Follow that course and you will be all right. I am speaking from experience when I say that the one who holds the liquor has no better outlook for the future here than he has in the old country. The one who can keep sober and work hard is on the way to prosperity. I have been in America four years and I have no more money than when I came here. All I have accumulated is a little experience. Yes, this is certain, there is no hope of success without complete abstinence."

He laid special emphasis on the last two words. A load of wheat arrived that Wang had to take care of and the conversation ended after an invitation by Wang for Ole to come back Sunday. "It gives me great pleasure to talk with you, and if I can help you in one way or another it would please me very much. I live upstairs in that building over there. Well then, goodnight!"

"What a fine person," thought Ole as he walked towards the bridge. "It would be a pity if drink were to take possession of him, but it does appear that it has."

The next Sunday Ole spent the entire day writing. He wrote a long letter to his parents giving the details of his travels, the work, the food and the customs as far as his short stay had revealed them to him. His new friend, Nils Wang, received a good mention. He expressed his joy over the hope that by fall he would have earned one hundred dollars and that he could send money home to them so they could buy their own food and clothes and pay the heavy debt to Bonden. Then he wrote a warm cheerful letter to Marie, full of dreams and plans.

Thursday night Ole went again to Carlton to mail the letters. There he saw Wang coming towards him, staggering out of a saloon. When he saw Ole in front of him he took him by the hand and said, "Drunk again! I don't know how this will end. Oh, if I were like you and could live over again seven of my worthless years!"

Large tears followed these words, and what came from the heart went straight to Ole's heart. He pitied the poor wretch. He had to part with Wang, however, when a drinking companion forcibly took him by the arm and dragged him back into the saloon. As he called goodbye to Ole he asked him to come over next Sunday.

So on Sunday Ole went to his rooms and found him in bed. "I am sick today," Wang greeted him. "And if not so much bodily, I fell ill in full measure mentally. This is always the way with me when I have been drinking a few days. Let me tell you something about my life, which, unfortunately does not have much of the bright side, especially the later years. My real name is Nils Pederson, but when I came over I changed it to Wang, my birthplace. I am from Ringerike in Norway on the east side of Tyrifjorden where so many legends and sagas have originated and where the sun rises on an enchanting valley, with islands in the fjord, surrounded by the community of Roisetangen. This valley my forebearers can claim as their own, where rich grainfields and meadows ripple under the gentle winds from the fjord. Many fine homes gleam among the heavily laden fruit orchards. There the old colossus, Jyruhaugen, stands silent and immovable, listening to and observing our culture, just as it stood far back in time when King Ring and Ingeborg in crossing the ice to go to a banquet at Vehold broke through into the water and were saved by Frithjof. Yes, I left this valley and my home for no other reason than an unhappy love affair. My eyes will never again see those dear places, forever impressed on my memory. My old parents, neither cotters or rich people, had sacrificed their all to give me a good schooling. They taught me faith in God and His Word. I completed school with first-rate marks and then my parents tried to get me to go to the Seminary, but it was my ambition to make a career in business. But when I had just gotten started, I unfortunately met a lovely, blue-eyed, amiable girl who won my heart completely. But if I live to be a thousand years I shall never know for certain why she had no love for me in return. At times in her correspondence there was evidence she loved me, which cut even deeper wounds in my heart when it proved to be only for a short while. When I determined at last that I would no longer be suspended between heaven and earth, I requested a definite answer from her. It gave me no hope and I fell into deepest misery. The ring I intended for her, and all the sweet memories, are lying on the bottom of Tyrifjord, and I might as well be lying there with them.

"Then I started my own mercantile business, which acquired a gilt-edge financial rating, name, and reputation. I was temperate and industrious, and while the youthful zest was left behind with my blue-eyed sweetheart, I nevertheless gave the same close attention to business and everything appeared to run smoothly. My business and social contracts were with the so-called 'better class' and I began to seek diversions. Since I felt that I was too old to be 'bottle-fed,' I accustomed myself to liquors by beginning with wine, then beer, and toddy."

"Soon I became acquainted with another girl who was a relative of the first one, but without her pleasing personality. I married her without love, which did not matter to her because she often said during our four years of married life that she did not love me either. For this both of us should probably be forgiven, for I found out that she was unsentimental and cold-hearted. Soon after our marriage it dawned on me that I had made a mistake and had sinned by using the holy state of matrimony and allowing the minister to perform the ceremony when the heart was not in tune. I had lied both before God and the minister who had so forcefully said, 'What God hath put together let no man put asunder'."

"More and more I sought consolation in drink. I expanded my business beyond the point justified by capital investment, and my credit, which was unrestricted, had to be used often so that eventually I could find no means to meet my obligations. The business began to go to pieces. I surrendered my home and about an equal amount from my assets, hoping to begin anew, but fate would not favor me. Again I started as an accountant with my former employer, but life soured on me when my 'friends' looked down on me with contempt. This happened not because I was given to drinking, although that would have been a very good reason, but rather because I now was poor. Disputes arose between me and my wife's family, who did not hesitate to take advantage of the situation and become unbearable. With my wife's consent, I said farewell forever to my fjords and islands and came over here, with the promise from my wife that she would join me in a year at the latest. At last I was here, full of good intentions, which were realized for a time as long as I abstained. I enjoyed the prospect of seeing my wife and two sons again, for even without love I had respect for my wife and our family relationship. But God knows if I ever shall see them again. It is clear that the bond between us was too loosely tied, and with my departure the knot fell apart, leaving each of us our separate lives."

Here Wang stopped his story. Ole had listened with keen attention and said to him, "But don't you think you could overcome the temptation if you had a faithful friend not addicted to drink, and you then avoided drinking companions?"

"Yes probably," Wang admitted. "I think that when I can go without the destructive stuff for weeks at a time, then the weeks can be lengthened into years, if it were not that a curse seems to be hanging over me as a punishment for my past."

"I can't believe that God punishes men by imposing drunkenness, unless for just a brief time to show its degrading effects and awaken a man's conscience," Ole ventured. "From now on let us be together and help each other -- you help me to speak English, and I will do all I can to drive out this evil within you."

They shook hands to seal their agreement, and from then on Ole visited his friend every Sunday, each time bringing along books of his own and some belonging to Klokker Aas. Little by little Wang appeared in better spirits. He saved some money, bought new clothes, and accompanied Ole to church every Sunday.

The middle of August Ole received letters from Norway and Nils Wang could understand the love he had for Marie. The letters expressed joy over his arrival in Quebec and avowed unfailing love.

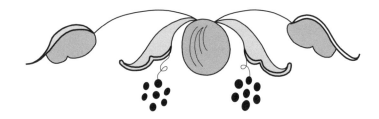

Chapter Twelve

Up On The Saeter

Now we will turn our attention to events in Sigdal, where autumn has come and all nature is attired in royal regalia. Fields have begun to ripen, billowing before the gentle winds; birches in their richest green double their glory by reflections in the enchanting Sigdal river. Hay is being cut and hay-stacks appear in the fields; orchards are laden with apples; berries redden among the leaves and flowers in the gardens. Under a bright sun the birds are singing, squirrels are leaping merrily among the branches or cracking nuts held in their paws, and the rabbits, frightened out of their bushes, stop to cock their ears for danger.

Marie Hovland saw and heard these things when she, on a beautiful Sunday, rode horseback up to the saeter. She had received a letter from Ole the day before. After going to Haugen to share her letter, and read the letter Torkil had received, she read her own letter to her mother. Since Gunhild was about to send food up to the saeter to Randi Haugen and Guri, she arranged it so that Marie could go there alone and Bonden would not know about the letters.

Marie arrived at the saeter before dinner and Randi was overjoyed to hear from her son; that he was contented, had a well-paying job, and would send them money that fall. Marie had permission to stay at the saeter until Monday and she helped the milkmaids with their chores. As they were having their evening meal, Guri, now well over fifty, began to display unusual gaiety and volunteered the news that she expected a suitor that evening, and the other two, who were now in high spirits, teased her until they all were laughing hilariously.

They went to bed, the three grownups in the large bed and the children in the smaller. But they did not go to sleep at once, for Guri told them stories about fairies, nisses, and hulder. She had been on the saeter thirty-seven summers and so she was as well acquainted with the hulder as with any human in the valley. They were completely harmless and full of fun, she assured them, and every time she gave the cow-call, or played on the lur, they were as sure to answer as Amen in church.

"If it were not for their long tails," she said, "you could not tell them from people. They have powerful influence over the weather, and if you treat them badly you can always be sure of lightning and thunder."

As Guri lay in bed and spun her stories, hoof-beats were heard passing over the heather and all listened breathlessly.

"Maybe it is a stray horse?"

"No, they never run about this time of night."

The thumping noise seemed to come nearer and sounded as it there were two or more horses. They thought they heard voices outside and in a few minutes there were knocks on the door. No one answered. The knocks continued, and a voice that sounded familiar called out, "Can you sell me some milk tonight? I am very thirsty."

"Who are you?" Guri asked.

"I am from Numedal. I am looking for horses that have strayed."

"God help us! I believe it is Asle Viig!" whispered Randi and Guri together.

"No, I cannot allow strangers in at this time of the night," Guri answered at last. "Perhaps I would if I knew you."

"You know me well enough, both of you and the others in there. Unlock this door! Don't you hear, you old gray goat!"

"Yes, now I think I can tell who you are by the fine language you use, but you cannot come inside no matter whether I am gray or white."

"Oh, take a joke, Guri. I didn't want to offend you, really. But tell me, is Marie Hovland in here?"

"No, she left for home this evening."

"Now you are lying, toothless woman, for just now I came from there. I shall come in even if I have to kick open the door, and I have permission from her father to do so. I have money to pay for it, even if I tore down the whole place. Marie! Will you come out, or shall I kick in the door?"

Then Guri whispered in Marie's ear, "Tell him you will come out to him in a minute, and I will put on your dress and go out in your place."

Marie gathered her courage and answered,

"It would not be becoming to let anyone come in here so late at night, but if you will promise not to tell a living soul I will come out to you."

This he promised on his honor.

Quickly Guri jumped up, slipped into Marie's pretty dress, stuffed in some old socks to fill in for the bosom, and put on a night cap. Then she went out, much to the joy of Marie and not to her own displeasure at that, for she had no objection to the amorous attentions of the valley's most attractive and promising young bachelor.

"How nice you are to come out here to me," he began.

"Hush! You must not talk so loud," whispered Guri, carrying a large bowl of milk with her out into the dark.

"Permit me to treat you in return. I have here a bottle of genuine Swedish Banko, really as sweet as you are yourself," he whispered, pressing her close to his breast as he soared up into Seventh Heaven.

"Thank you, but it is not customary for girls to drink anything so strong."

"Oh tut, there is no one to see us here anyway." He took the flask out of his pocket, took a swig himself, and gave it to Guri with these words, "Take a good dram. It shall seal our engagement -- skaal -- not so?"

"Yes if you love me and your intentions are honest," returned Guri, taking the bottle.

"Here is my hand on that. Warmer love and affection than I have for you cannot be found. You must definitely have forgotten the cotter's son, so I can surely count on your love in return. Yes, I can tell there is a change in you. You used to act as if you were too good to talk to me, although I did not consider myself to be an outcast of society."

"I have liked the cotter's boy as a good and kind friend, that is all, and so it will be an easy thing to forget him. If it is your honest intention, you know I would consider myself lucky to be your wife."

"Yes it is my honest intention, my golden one," he replied tenderly. "Who should want to lie to an angel like you?" he added as his lips softly met hers.

He sat down on a stump by the wall, took her in his lap with his right hand, and his left he placed over her soft bosom.

"Will you permit me to whistle for my friend, Einar Holst, the clerk in Berg's store. You know him. He brought sugar and raisins, and maybe a little bottle too."

"No, dear Asle, do not mention the bottle again. You can understand that it is unbecoming for young girls to drink."

"Oh no, I meant to take only a sip to quench my thirst and to keep us awake."

Asle whistled, and a tall lanky fellow, who began to bow and show off, greeted them politely, "Good evening Jomfru Hovland, with whom I presume I have the honor to stand face to face, without seeing you in the darkness. Oh, for a pair of cat's eyes! But I may be disturbing you?"

"No, but don't talk so loud, my long-legged friend," Asle whispered and gave him a punch.

Jomfruen, too, assured Holst that there was no disturbance.

"Here is a big cup," Asle whispered, giving him the empty milk bowl.

Holst emptied the contents of the bottle into the bowl and asked, "How can we divide this evenly?" offering it to the Jomfru first.

Guri, like many other older women, did not refuse a drink and very likely took her share. Asle also drank, and then Holst took the bowl as he said, "Here's to the free and happy saeter life and the company of angels! If there be a creature who deserves to be called an angel, it is surely Jomfru Hovland. May I be permitted to extend congratulations? From what I hear I understand that Asle has come off victorious."

"Yes, the girl is mine!" said Asle, and Holst caught the sound of a kiss. "If you don't believe me, you will surely believe her."

"Of course, I am proud to be his sweetheart," whispered the Jomfru.

"Congratulations and best wishes," Holst toasted them. "May you go through life as in a dance until gray hairs appear. And so, bottoms up!"

"I hope you will excuse me," whispered the presumed Jomfru Hovland. "I must go, or the girls may start a lot of gossip about me. Please do, and save me the embarrassment!"

"But you shall have something as a first present," insisted Asle. "Here, take my watch. I'll soon be going to Drammen, where I will buy you a fine young lady's watch and reclaim this one."

Guri accepted the gift, but regretted that she had nothing to give in return.

"Do give me a lock of your beautiful brown hair," pleaded Asle. "I shall keep it as something sacred, more precious to me than gold or silver."

"With pleasure, you may have it," answered Guri. "If only I can find my scissors in the dark."

"I am a store clerk and always carry scissors in my pocket," volunteered Holst. "Would you want to use them?"

Guri chuckled inwardly as she clipped a bit of hair from what little she had left under her nightcap, with no guarantee implied as to the color, and gave it to Alse. Then she said farewell to Holst, who left her a present of something from a bag from his store.

Asle and Guri parted after a warm embrace without further words, for "When the heart speaks loudest, the tongue is silent." All nature was sleep and so quiet that the Jomfru could count the heart beats of her admirer without feeling them at all as they were clasped together -- the stockings were insulation.

Soon Asle was able to talk again and he thanked her for saving his life, for without her, life would be impossible, he declared. He bid her an affectionate goodbye and rode away in high spirits, elated over his triumphant courting. On his speedy horse Sleipner he quickly overtook Holst.

Guri returned to the hut bursting with

laughter, and assured them that never in her life had she been so important or so high in favor. She talked as if she were intoxicated, and the others laughed with her.

"I am engaged to Asle," she reported. "I have had kisses and caresses, Swedish Banko and port wine, sugar and raisins. Berg's clerk called me Jomfru and spoke to me as politely as if I were a queen. He proposed a toast to us and said we should be 'conscrapulated,' whatever that means. These fine city words I don't understand. Asle gave me his watch. Listen, it goes tick, tick, tick."

"But will this give me a bad reputation in the valley?" Marie interposed, worriedly.

"That will all be cleared up in the morning, for as soon as he sees the lock of my hair which I gave him, it will be clear that you are not involved," Guri assured her. All laughed until the walls of the hut shook and there was little sleep for them that night. Old Guri added to the festivity by treating sugar and raisins.

Chapter Thirteen

Broken Hope

The merriment which took place on the saeter over in Norway was, sad to say, a prelude to later sorrows and disappointments on both sides of the ocean. Ole was very happy and satisfied. He had received letters from Norway, the bridge would soon be finished, and he expected them to receive his wages. While the Irish entertained themselves with fighting and swearing, Ole was looking forward to the time when he could make his parents happy by sending them eighty dollars of his pay.

The day the bridge was finished, the engineers came and accepted the job, after which the contractor received his payment and then paid off his workmen. When he came to Ole he said, "You have been one of my best and most trustworthy men. I would like to have you remain another week to help put the company's machinery in condition."

Ole agreed to the offer for it would put nine more dollars in his pocket. Burke, the contractor, therefore did not care to carry so much on his person when he was working.

With only one day's work left, Burke gave Ole orders for the completion of the job and left him, saying that he had to go to Carlton with certain letters. On arriving home for dinner Ole noticed the contractor had not returned, but thought nothing of it, assuming that Burke was busy at his home and with some lots he owned in Carlton. However, when Burke did not return that night, Ole began to suspect trouble, and early the next morning went in to the city.

What he learned made Ole furious and left him heartbroken. He found that Burke had sold his Carlton property several weeks ago, and that he had left the city the day before without anyone knowing where he had gone. In his distress Ole turned to Nils Wang for help and consolation, and Nils tried to locate Burke by telegraphing to various places, but without results. It was as if Burke had sunk into the ground.

This was a hard blow for Ole. He had worked faithfully, both when Burke was around and in his absence, even to the last hour. Throughout the fall he had thought and dreamed so much about the happiness that awaited his parents when they would get the money, all of which was in one stroke blotted out. He was without a cent in his pocket and knew of no place to turn to get work now that harvest time was just ending.

"Oh, if only I were back in the cottage at Haugen," he sighed. "Or if a bridge stretched from America to Norway, I would start walking this minute."

It appeared that Ole would give up in despair and Wang tried without result to console him by suggesting that he take his misfortune calmly and stay with him over the winter. He could earn a living by chopping wood, and could stay with him, he suggested. But Ole would not agree. "I am going to a logging camp even if I have to walk," he declared, "for I have more than just myself to think of," and he broke into tears. "If you will let me leave my trunk in your room, I will start on foot. I'll get there somehow."

"Yes, but the nearest pine forests are more than one hundred and fifty miles to the north, and it will take you a week to reach them," Nils warned. "Furthermore you will run into many difficulties; no railroads, few roads, rivers to cross, with neither boats nor bridges, and many desolate places where you will find neither food nor housing. I don't want to stop you there now, earning money, but I think it is my duty to call your attention to the impossible conditions you will be up against to get there. I know this country, Ole."

As Wang talked, Ole stood silently and listened. Finally he said, "I am determined to challenge any danger or difficulty to reach the logging camp. It isn't very cold yet, and the roads over the prairies are dry and easy to walk. I will take nothing with me but working clothes, so I shall not be loaded down and can make time traveling."

He immediately went for his trunk and brought it to Wang's for storage. Wang made him take two dollars, the last he had, and they promised to write to each other. Then Ole was on his way.

Chapter Fourteen

Worse And Worse

It was soon time for supper, and the warm sun that had shot its last beams over the prairies now mixed with the cold northwest winds. Ole relied on the compass Wang had given him to set his course in a northeasterly direction through wild territory, towards the town of Kingston in Wisconsin, some fifty miles away.

A little after sundown he fortunately reached a farm house, where he received permission from the farmer to stop overnight. He had then made sixteen miles of his journey in one day. After paying a half-dollar to the farmer for the night, Ole started early and strode over the wide expanse of prairie, where he could walk unhindered. He made good time until he came to a river. He followed the bank up and down but could not find a road, house, boat or bridge. After some time he discovered a fallen log by the edge of the river and he worked with it for a time to get it loose, but the log was frozen to the ground so solidly that he could not budge it. Then he said to himself, "I must cross!" and disregarding the cold fall weather he undressed rapidly, bundled his clothes, bound them on his back with his suspenders, and, after getting cramps, he ran into the water and swam across the hundred-foot wide river. Quickly he put on his clothes, but his shoes were not there. He searched along the shore with no success, and it seemed certain they they must have fallen into the water and floated downstream. So he put his stockings in his pocket and continued the journey barefooted. Very soon his feet became cold from the water dripping off his soaked clothes. Then deciding it was better to ruin the socks than his health, he put the socks on, and by running kept his feet warm.

Soon he came to a road which, according to the compass, led in the direction of Kingston. Considerably cheered, he followed the road and began to run again. Hearing a sound back of him, he looked around and was happy to see someone coming down the road in his direction and would soon catch up to him. As he stepped to the side of the road, one of the men pointed a revolver at him, calling out, "You are my prisoner!"

The driver brought the horses to a halt, one man jumped out of the wagon and put handcuffs on Ole, while the one with the gun held it on him until Ole's hands were shackled. Then they searched Ole, took what he had in his pockets and forced him to climb into the wagon. The horses were turned around, and they returned the same way they had come. The two men engaged in conversation and at last one of them said to Ole, "Didn't you even have time to put on your shoes when you left Janesville jail today?"

"I have never been in Janesville. I came from Carlton."

"Nonsense! It won't help you any to deny it. Do you think that anyone with a grain of sense would run off in his stocking feet this time of the year? No, it's evident that you were escaping from Janesville, and before you get back you will regret that you left your shoes. It's cold enough with them on today."

"But don't you see my clothes are wet?"

Ole began, his words heavy with Norwegian accent. "I swam the river over there with my clothes in a bundle on my back, and my shoes fell out. If anyone has done anything wrong in Janesville, as you are saying, then you must have some idea as to what nationality he is. From the papers you have taken from me, I can prove that I am Norwegian, that I was in Carlton yesterday, and I think it is your duty to examine the case a little before you arrest anyone in suspicion. When I was running directly ahead, I could have found hiding places enough if I had wanted to. On the contrary, I was glad to see people on these prairies and expected no trouble as I have done no wrong."

The men stopped their horses, and one remarked to the others, "He does not talk like an Irishman, more like a Norseman. But the description fits perfectly. Look through his papers."

Handcuffed, Ole had to stand helplessly and watch the men tear open his precious papers and the letters from his parents and Marie. The last photograph he had received fell out of the envelope to the floor of the wet wagon, where it lay so that Marie's face smiled up at him, giving him strength enough to have broken his chains. But he forced himself to be calm, and hoped that the men would set him free.

"Pick up the photograph, at least!" Ole demanded, which they did immediately and then exclaimed as they looked at the picture, "She is beautiful! Like an angel!" They raved on and on, then one of them said, "You are Norwegian as we can see by the cancellation stamp on this envelope. But we don't understand what is written."

Ole answered, "I am Norwegian, and, furthermore, there is a letter of recommendation among my papers from a merchant in Carlton directed to the Pinery Company at Green Bay, Wisconsin, which will show by the date that I was in Carlton yesterday."

They found it, and from their conversations he learned that the robber they were after had been in Janesville the whole week. Ole was then freed from their custody, but, he was four miles back of the place where the officers had arrested him. The sun was now low in the west and his cold limbs refused to carry him further. Only with determined effort to exert himself could he get up a trot. At last he was back at the place where he had been arrested, but he felt so

exhausted that he had to slacken his speed.
After he had gone a mile or two he saw
smoke rising among the trees, but suddenly
his joy turned to fear for he had approached
so near to an Indian camp that two Indians
had trained their guns on him. They raised
their guns as a sign of peace, but Ole did not
understand the meaning of the gesture.
Nevertheless, he went toward them and
thought that if they wanted to kill him they
could do so now. When Ole realized that
they were friendly, he pointed to his bare feet
and took a dollar out of his pocket. One of
the Indians went into a tent and came out
with a pair of buckskin moccasins, making
signs for more money. Then Ole took out his
last half-dollar but the Indian shook his head
holding up two fingers. The deal was made,
however, when Ole turned his pockets inside
out.

They asked him to come into one of the
tents, which Ole was glad to do, and there
he found a fire to warm his feet and body,
and he put on the moccasins. He named the
town of Kingston, holding up his fingers, and
one Indian seemed to understand, for he nod-
ded and held up nine fingers, which Ole
interpreted to mean nine miles. He hesitated

no longer and left the camp to continue his journey, now without a cent in his pocket.

It was dark when he reached Kingston, where he hoped to get some much needed rest, but he was reluctant to ask for lodging without money. On inquiry his found that there was a Norwegian, Chris Olson, who owned a hotel. He went to see him, but at first glance he knew that the man before him was as hard and unsympathetic as Bonden at Hovland. Ole asked, "I came here to see if I could stay overnight."

"Yes, that can be arranged."

"But, I have no money."

"If you have no money, you cannot stay here. You'll have to be satisfied to sleep outside like the other tramps. Men who work have money at this time of the year," the innkeeper told him coldly.

"I have worked ever since I came from Norway this summer, but I received no pay because the contractor ran away with my money."

"Yes, bums like you usually cook up some excuse. I have been in the hotel business over twelve years and I've had experience with them. Do you have any suitcase or something else with you to leave here?"

The Cotter's Son

"No, I left my clothing in Carlton because I decided to go on foot all the way to the Pineries."

"I suppose you have left your money there too, probably at some saloon. I have no sympathy for you, smart fellow."

"Well, do as you please," answered Ole as he went out. "Should I ever meet you again it shall be a pleasure to return the compliments."

He continued in the same northwesterly direction toward a forest he could see in the distance. In low spirit, he thought about why he had come to this country -- to earn enough to go back to Norway to establish a home. "Risk all to attain this goal," Mother Hovland had said to him. And too, he needed money to aid his parents, threatened with want. These were the motives for his journey, which in the beginning promised so much. But how bitter the disappointment! Especially did he feel it this evening, when he was tired and hungry, without a cent in his pocket, and suspected as a thief and a vagabond who did not want to work. His hands bore evidence that he had worked and worked hard. Now he knew not where he could spend the night. "If I don't find a farm house," he thought, "it will be necessary to keep going the whole night, for to lie down in the cold night with nothing but my thin clothes on would be sure death."

As he walked on, dejected and miserable, he was cheered by a rising full moon that gleamed over the tree tops, and he knew he would have light for his journey. Then he remembered that a moon just like this one served him well when he once was sitting on a stone in the corner of the rose garden at Hovland, writing a poem to Marie in which he wished for wings to fly to her room. "Oh, if I only had wings now," he signed to himself, as tears rose to his eyes.

After he had reached a hill about three miles from Kingston, he saw a light to his left. He changed his course towards it, hoping that it might be a light in a farm house where he might be permitted to sleep in the hay overnight. When he reached the foot of the hill, the light disappeared, but he kept on in the same direction, in spite of many hindrances, including swampy ground and small streams, where the ice was so thin to carry him, so that he had to wade through ice and water up to his knees, being too weak to jump. After about an hour he stopped and began to doubt that he had followed the right course towards the light, which he had not seen since leaving the foot of the hill. It could not have been as far away as the distance he had walked, he judged. "By this time, perhaps, it is so late that all have gone to bed. Lucky is the one who has his house and can go to rest," Ole sighed. He decided that now there was no other way than to locate a woodland where he would be shielded against the biting wind, and he would then continue walking all night. The water of the streams washed the blood from his sore feet in the sloshing moccasins.

Soon he saw trees and made his way through the long grass and brush into the woods, where he found relief from the wind. Occasionally he frightened a wild animal from its lair, which he could hear but not see. Not only was he tired and footsore, but he began to feel dull and sleepy, as if he did not care any longer. Afraid that he would go to sleep under the open sky, he began to gather grass as fast as his remaining energy would allow to make a bed before he fell asleep. The last he remembered was a vivid dream in which he saw Marie and his mother and Guri lie down in the same manner as he did, on hay and under the open sky. Marie cried, and his mother stroked her cheeks. A short time after he visioned a tall man and a lean man ride away, and the hay on which the women lay was on fire. Frightened, Ole awoke, stiff and sold as ice. He tried to rise but could not stay on his feet, now no longer tender and sore. They were now without feeling. It was daylight and he could see smoke ahead of him after he had crawled about in the woods for half and hour. He realized that he was now four or five miles from the hill where he saw the light first and the smoke was about halfway between.

He crawled out of the woods and over the white-frosted prairie about the same way as he came. The cold night had done some good because the stream had ice on it thick enough for him to crawl over without falling through. The ice held his weight until he reached the grassy edge on the other side, where he fell through. Then it dawned on him that cold water was a remedy for frozen feet. He held them in the water for awhile and then exerted himself to the utmost to move and bend them. Feeling came back to his feet, but God knows that they were far from good. Now he was limbered up enough to stand erect, and he continued walking, though slowly and unsteadily.

Gradually Ole approached the smoke, then he saw the chimney, then the roof, and soon there rose before him a large two-story farm-house with many outbuildings. Painfully he reached the steps to the door of the kitchen and crawled up to the door and knocked. A woman opened the door, and astonished at the sight of him, she ran to the woodshed and soon came back with two men. With great difficulty Ole told them of his plight, and the farmer, a Mr. Williams, realizing the situation immediately, went in and brought out some medicine to give him, while his wife and a black-haired girl began to unlace and remove his moccasins. A larger girl came carrying a bundle of clothes on her arm, and laid them in a side-room where, with the help of Mr. Williams, Ole took off his wet clothes and put on the dry garments. Removing his stockings was a painful and dif-ficult job, for they were glued to his feet with blood and ice. Williams shook his head, mumbled something to himself, and went to get a bottle, the contents of which he applied to Ole's feet. Then he left the house, and Ole saw him drive away in a buggy.

Breakfast was prepared for him, but all he could swallow was a cup of coffee. As he sat by the table he could barely understand what the girl was saying to her mother, "I would give the seven dollars I've got in the bank if the doctor can make him well!" From this, Ole knew Williams had gone for a doctor. In an hour Williams did return, accompanied by Dr. Jones from Kingston. He brought medicine, and ordered Ole to bed. As he was helped up the stairs Ole said, "As I told you this morning, I have no money to pay for this."

"The county has money," Williams answered, "and if not, I have. You shall not die from neglect. We need many more such as you in this country. When I first saw you lying on my steps and you told your story, I noticed callouses on your hands, which you can get in no other way than by hard work. Anyone can see that you are not a drunkard, so you deserve all the help we can give you. Take courage, you will be well again before the week is over."

The doctor encouraged him too and asked him to stop worrying, for now he would be happy in the hands of these good people, receive good care, and soon be well again.

But it was the girl's words to her mother and the smile on Williams' face that moved Ole to tears, and he whispered more distinctly than before, so that everyone could hear, "I can never repay you for all you have done for me."

Chapter Fifteen

An Unhappy Engagement Party

When we left the people of Sigdal, everyone there was happy enough, but now as we return the situation is quite changed.

As soon as Asle Viig awoke Monday morning after his visit to the saeter, he went down and told his parents that he was now definitely engaged to Marie Hovland and that he wanted to get married, the sooner the better. His father answered him saying, "You are yet too young to be married. You need more experience."

"That may be so," said Asle, as he scratched his ear, "but girls are as undependable as wild birds, and they must be kept in a cage to be sure about them. If the cotter's son should come back and write poetry to her again, he might put ideas into her head."

"Oh, have no fear of that," his mother said. "Marie is as dependable as the earth she stands on, and if she has given a promise to you seriously, with faith and honor, she will not deceive you, even if you postponed the wedding ten years. But, to make it doubly sure, you can have your engagement party publicly next Sunday, for all who want to come. You will make certain that no one else will come and ask for the girl. You have her parents on your side, and Marie has always been a dear friend of yours. You surely remember that her father told you this when he was here on Christmas Day."

Summons were sent to the cotter's wives, and the whole week they were busy washing clothes, brewing, baking, and cleaning, in preparing for the engagement banquet. Asle himself personally invited all the most promi-nent families, including those of Strøm and Holst. Holst was even given the honor of delivering the engagement toast at the ban-quet, on the composing of which he spent the whole week.

When Asle arrived at Hovland, he revealed his errand only to Bonden and asked that everyone come over Sunday for coffee.

He told him of the confidential talk he had with Marie at the saeter and added that she was not the same girl, now that the cotter's son was out of her mind.

"Oh, that was only puppy-love between them," answered Bonden. "I always thought that you would come out the winner in the end, for the girl could not wish herself a better husband."

More courteous than was his wont, and also sober, Asle greeted Gunhild and Marie in the living room of the Hovland home. He favored the latter with amorous glances, which she did not acknowledge. "How bashful she still is," he thought, "but in the dark she is different."

After Asle had gone, Bonden told his wife and daughter that the family had been invited over to Viig the coming Sunday. "They are having a party to honor Mother Viig on her birthday," he said, thinking Marie might be timid and would refuse to go if he told her the facts.

Sunday afternoon Marie had a headache and went to bed, but she could not escape her father. She had to get out in the fresh air, he insisted, and then she would soon feel better. So she dressed and went with her parents in their new carriage to Viig.

Darkness was closing in when they arrived at the Viig home. A servant took charge of the horses as Asle and Thore helped the guests out of their carriage.

"Good evening and thank you," Torsten Hovland said in greeting, to which his host responded, "Welcome and thanks to you." And as Thore Viig took Marie's hand he said, "So you are going to be my daughter-in-law!"

"I am not that yet," she answered, as she passed on to shake hands with Gunhild.

In the parlor, many whispered remarks and greetings followed. The guests were taken to a side-room to remove their wraps. Back in the parlor, Gunhild and Marie were treated to wine and cake, and Torsten had a glass of stronger stimulant. Holst sat busily thinking and chewing his mustache, while Asle waited with eager anticipation to hear a fine and eloquent tribute to Marie and himself. Marie sat by her mother's side in the seat of honor, silent and apparently worried.

When the coffee was being served, Asle drew his chair over to Marie and whispered, "How have you been this week?"

"As usual, thank you."

"That's good, I'm so happy. Will you swap

watches today?"

"No, I am not doing any trading."

"That I know well enough, but the one I gave you is too large for you, so here I have a smaller one."

Marie was puzzled as to what answer to make, so she said nothing. However, she gave Asle a look which he interpreted to mean that it was not proper to talk about such things in front of the guests. She then turned to her mother to break the unpleasant conversation, an act that Asle credited to modesty. The thought went through Marie's troubled mind, "I wonder if he has not seen the lock of hair yet?"

After coffee the punchbowl was brought out. The aroma alone seemed to influence many of the guests. Soon each had his glass, and the supreme moment had come. Holst arose with glass in hand, coughed, and looked over to Asle, who rose and went over to seat himself next to Marie. He made an awkward bow before her and took her hand, but she jerked it out of his grasp.

"Come now! Stand up! Take heart, my dear, and Holst will propose the engagement toast for us!" he whispered.

"Then you will have to see to it that you

have your betrothed here," Marie whispered back in embarrassment.

"I have no other than you, and any other I would not wish for," said Asle.

"Then you are surely without one," Marie flashed back.

Then Torsten Hovland came over to Marie and asked what was the matter with her.

"Oh, nothing! If only Asle will leave me alone," she said out loud, so all heard it.

"Oh, he will not offend you, my child. If you don't want to stand up, Asle can come and sit down by you."

Asle sat down and Holst began his toast in a dignified tone of voice. "My dear ladies and gentlemen! All your undertakings in the world, small or large, have two inescapable parts, namely, a beginning and an end. What attracts us to this festive party is this; the son of this home, my friend Asle Viig, has found one who has sworn to be his faithful companion through life. As this is the betrothal, or the beginning of their life together, he has invited friends and neighbors to come and be joyful with him. My friend, you have been fortunate in your choice. Lucky is the man with an angel like her by his side to accompany him on life's journey. I will repeat the words I said last Sunday -- the wish that your way through life may be strewn with roses, that you may have health and strength to the end of life, that you may be happy all your days. And to Jomfru Hovland, who can look forward into a future filled with joy with a man like Asle Viig with ---"

At this Marie interrupted him. She rose and said, "You must pardon me for interrupting your speech, but when my name is included therein I believe you must have obtained the wrong information, for I have never sworn Asle Viig my troth and I shall never do so."

"What are you saying!" Asle burst forth angrily, "I thought a while ago that you just showed your silly bashfulness, but now this has gone too far. Why did you promise so faithfully on the saeter last Sunday to be my betrothed when you can't keep faith for a week?"

"I did not talk with you on Sunday."

"You can't deny that you did, for Holst was with me, and he can bear witness to it."

He looked over to Holst, who had become so confused that the rest of his speech had completely failed him. However, he put forth his best effort and said, "Yes, I heard Jomfro

Hovland say that she felt proud that she could call you 'My betrothed'."

"Did you see me out there?" Marie demanded.

"No, I didn't exactly, but Asle Viig can produce evidence, for you gave each other gifts."

"That is right!" Asle broke in, with a glow of satisfaction spreading over his face. He rushed up to his room and came back with a folded piece of paper in his hand. He walked over to Marie and said in an overbearing manner, "Were you not outside the saeter hut last Sunday night? You brought out a bowl of milk, drank from my bottle, sat on my lap, and declared that you never were in love with the cotter's son, but that you would belong to me until death, and then you received my pocket watch as a pledge."

Marie answered just as positively, "No, either you dreamed it, or some other girl has fooled you!"

"I will prove to you that I am neither dreaming nor letting any girl fool me for I know both your dress and your voice. Because it was dark, I was thoughtful enough, although I could never mistrust you, to get a lock of your hair. Here before everyone I shall show you that all may see the proof that you yourself were with me, and not some other girl."

Thore Viig and Torsten Hovland moved nearer to the table, and Holst too turned eager eyes upon them as Asle opened the paper and took out a lock of hair that unfortunately had faded and had turned light gray.

Asle looked like one struck by lightening, and -- as after a thunderbolt -- everyone was silent. Strøm and Holst struggled to keep back their laughter. But Asle burst out with a flood of his most-used oaths, scratched his ear with one hand, and lifted his glass with the other. He drank it down, and the others followed his example. Then Asle turned to Torsten Hovland and said, "You think you can make a fool of me up at your saeter, but I swear that you shall rue the trick in the end. I shall get both of those toothless witches of yours locked up and fed bread and water. Yes, this very week! But listen, my friends, inasmuch as we are together we shall have a good time anyway. Fill your glasses, and fill them again, and later we'll play a round of cards. I'll show them I will not eat my heart out for a bagatelle of a girl, for of such there is not only a handful but a whole landful, we all know that."

"This is an unpleasant affair," Torsten Hovland said, as he turned to Asle and emptied his third glass of punch. "But to whom do you think you spoke? Couldn't you see her?"

"No, it was dark as pitch," Asle said, "and I was warned not to use matches. But whoever it was, I will wager Sleipner that she was not wearing a cotter's dress, nor do I think it was any of those dried up scarecrows who are working for you up there, for she was a buxom woman. From her voice I could not tell a thing for we were whispering all the time."

Torsten rose and went into the sitting room, where Marie and her mother were waiting, and asked in a domineering tone of voice, "Were you not out talking with Asle last Sunday night on the saeter?"

"No," said Marie.

"Who was it, then?"

"That undoubtedly the hair will determine."

"I asked you who it was. Don't you realize I am your father?"

"It was Guri who went outside.."

"Dear Torsten," Gunhild interposed, for

she could see that Bonden was furious and very drunk, "be patient until we find out all that happened. Maybe the girl is not to blame as much as you think."

"And so you are going to interfere now," Bonden lashed out at his wife, "you who said you were so sick all week, unable to speak, and had to keep quiet. I do not wish to argue any longer here before all these people. Neither you nor the girl is going to ruin my good name and reputation however much you try. The question now is -- will you, Marie, come on bended knee and beg pardon from Asle or get out of the house this very minute, both you and your mother. I don't think the Viig folks will make any further claims on you. I have done everything possible to give you a good education. I have not spared a shilling to give you anything that would gladden your heart, and I have dressed you fit to be present with kings and queens without embarrassment, and the only thanks or return I ask is that you deport yourself so that I may be proud and happy. But instead you resist my wishes and bring me only shame and sorrow. And what was it you did before confirmation? Gave away money I sent with you for the minister, and then you took the side of the criminal so that he went free. I have not chastised you before for this. I wished to be forbearing with you inasmuch as you were but a child. Now, however, since you continue your obstinacy into womanhood my patience is at an end, and I want you to understand that I do not spend money on you for frills, so as to be admired by the cotter's son. If you take him seriously -- and I understand that he has inspired you with fancies that you cannot get out of your head -- then I say that you will find out when it is too late that you do not have me to come to for help. If it should come to the point that you sat without a mouthful of food in a cottage you may well die before you receive any help from me. Now will you go with Asle?"

"No," replied Marie firmly. "However much I admit that I am obligated to you for what you have done for me, and however faithfully I wish as your daughter to obey your commands, this is for me impossible."

"Then, leave this place if that is what you like better, but remember, you shall account for your stubbornness sometime, if not in the presence of all these people here tonight."

Bonden went over to a card table and sat down. Mother Hovland and Marie took their wraps and quietly left through the kitchen.

"Where has Marie gone?" Asle asked Bonden, entering the room.

"She went upstairs to lie down for awhile," Bonden replied. "She complained of a headache, but I think it's more likely that she has a guilty conscience."

Half an hour later Gunhild and Marie had nearly reached Hovland. They slowed up a bit to catch their breath, for they had been running all the way across the fields, with their wraps slung over their arms, in too much of a hurry even to put them on, fearing that they might be overtaken. Marie said, "I am afraid someone may be chasing us when they discover we have left, I don't know where we can hide."

"Your father won't be back before day-break, for he sat down to a card game," said Gunhild. "Likely he will be drunk when he comes and will begin abusing you again -- perhaps worse. It might be better for you to go over to Lie before sunrise and stay with father and mother for a few days."

"Oh mother, let me rather go up to the saeter as soon as possible, for I am afraid Asle will be coming over here tonight!"

"You may, if you think you could find your

way in the dark. It would be best to wake Erick and have him get you a horse," Gunhild said as they reached the door.

While Erick saddled Blakken, Marie changed clothes, and on returning mounted the horse and disappeared in the darkness. She reached the saeter before midnight, led the horses into the corral, and to her great relief Randi let her in. Sobbing and talking at the same time, she told all about the trouble she was in, while Randi listened and tried to comfort her, without result. Guri did not awaken and continued to sleep, snoring loudly.

"I am between the bark and the wood," Marie wept, "and whichever way I turn I will be in trouble. As things are now, everything I do is contrary to my father's wishes and stirs his anger. To obey him is impossible. I would rather choose death, consoling myself with Ole's last words when he left, 'Our wedding shall be consumated in heaven'."

Randi went to bed and was soon asleep, but Marie was unable to get a wink of sleep. About two o'clock, noticing a peculiar odor in the hut, she rose and went to the fireplace, but saw no fire there, nor in the clothes hanging nearby. She went back to bed and tried to sleep, but her troubled thoughts kept her awake. Then she became aware of a crackling and rumbling outside the door, and fire and smoke came in through the cracks between the logs. She leaped out of bed and quickly awakened the sleeping women, four in all, including Randi's four-year-old twins. Half-dressed, they tried to open the door, but the heat drove them back. Already the flames were lapping through the half-burned door. They tried to open the window and found it nailed shut, so quickly they took up a heavy stick of wood, broke the window open, and crawled out one after the other, not daring to take time to bring a thing with them.

No sooner was Marie out than she threw up her arms, and shrieked, "I left Ole's letters and photographs under my pillow, I must have them or die!"

Randi tried to hold her back, but she broke away and crawled back through the open window, fumbled around in the smoke, and finding the treasures, crawled out through the window, her hair singed. That instant the roof dropped, but luckily she cleared the falling timbers. Her clothes caught fire, however, and they were extinguished only with great difficulty, as no water was to be had.

It was a fearful night for the poor people. Cows lowed and the oxen bellowed, birds that had been sleeping in the trees around the hut were flying frantically about, adding to the bedlam.

Fortunately, it was a warm night, so the women and children could sit down on the ground. But what to do! Everything was destroyed in the fire, and only a smoking pile of ashes remained. In a shocked state they tried to figure out how the fire could have started, whether by accident or on purpose. There was evidence of partly burned newspapers scattered about by the wind, also some partly burned sticks that had been brought there after they had gone to bed. Later they found prints from a man's shoes in the sandy road, and the picture of Asle Viig inevitably came to mind.

When the day broke, Guri went down to Hovland to tell the bad news and to get food and clothes for the women who remained on the saeter with the herd. During the day Marie found a small, shiny key.

Bonden returned from Viig, immoderately intoxicated. Being told what had happened, he flew into a rage and declared that the fire was caused by the carelessness of the women. He rode immediately up to the saeter, and as soon as he saw Marie he ordered her to go home. Then he informed Randi that she and her family must leave Haugen. The cotter's contract had terminated many years ago and was invalid so that she would have to find herself another home.

So Randi took her hymn book, the only article she had saved from the fire, and tucked it in her bosom -- and taking the twins by the hand she began the slow, weary walk home, where she had so often gone in happier moods. Her tears flowed freely, and so fixed were these thoughts that she did not notice little Peder and Guri complain of hunger, having had no breakfast.

Soon, Marie, riding her horse, Blakken, overtook them and joined Randi in person and in thought, for she was as unhappy as Randi.

"I wonder how this will end?" Marie sighed after a long pause. "Were it not for poor mother, I would much prefer to go to some village or city and work hard for my living rather than stay here. And poor you! I -- " Her voice choked and prevented her from saying any more.

"There is no way out for us other than to unload ourselves at Svartbraaten," moaned Randi. "We may be able to get some harvest work during the fall, either at Sven Lie's or some other place. But I don't see how we can manage through the winter. If Ole only had not written and promised us money in the fall!"

Soon they arrived at the fork in the road where they must part. Randi extended her hand to Marie, who gave it a firm squeeze. Then with a parting look, each went silently on her way.

The Haugen cottage was small and miserable, but it had been home for the Haugen folks for twenty years. There were so many precious memories that had become a part of it, even before they were married, when Torkil had built the place. As he worked, he had dreamed of his coming marriage to Randi and their happy family life ahead of them.

When Randi arrived at the hut she discovered all its contents lying helter-skelter among the rocks outside. Her dresser, which she had inherited, lay at the front steps, and a broken drawer lay on he ground. Her wedding dress and bouquet had been dumped out and lay on the steps before the nailed up door. Though the bouquet was withered, the memories it held were fresh. Sadly she let it lie, rather than pick it up and have it fall to pieces. The twins cried and pushed repeatedly on the door, begging their mother to open it and give them something to eat. She tried to quiet them and promised them something soon, but then she remembered that she had nothing to give them.

While she was still sitting there picking myrtle leaves from the bouquet, Torkil appeared, slowly trudging up the hill with little Margarete. She was eleven years old now, and well understood their pitiful situation. Randi loved her, as she did her other children, perhaps a little more because she resembled Ole so much. Now she realized with a shock that Bonden's support had been withdrawn from Gunhild Hovland's plans for the girl's education. Margarete resembled Ole in mentality as well as appearance, and gave great promise, but because of Bonden's attitude they would have to give up hopes for her education.

Torkil was dismayed when he saw the bouquet, the dress and the nailed door, and he shook his head sadly as he looked at their possessions strewn about. Quietly he said, "Here we are together but homeless. Tell me about the fire up on the saeter?"

"Someone started it," Randi said. "We have positive evidence of that. While it is hard to say, it very likely was Asle Viig who wanted to avenge himself on Guri." Then she told about all that had happened the previous Sunday. The twins, Peder and Guri, refused to leave their home without food, so the parents had to carry them away, together with some of the smaller articles. Dejectedly they set out for Svartbraaten, where they were housed temporarily.

As soon as Marie arrived home, her father took her into the house for a talk with her. He said that he well knew that she was the cause of the fire, or had talked others into setting fire to the saeter hut. For what else would she be doing up there in the middle of the night? He said he saw two reasons for her act. One could be revenge because he had reprimanded her the evening before. The other might be an attempt to put the blame on Asle, so as to create enmity between himself and Asle, thus preventing his efforts to have her marry Asle. To blame Asle for the crime would be fruitless, he declared, for he has more than twenty witnesses that he did not leave the house that night.

"So now there is no longer any other way out for you than to marry Asle Viig before the coming Christmas, or be sent to prison. If you dare refuse this time, then not only will you suffer but you will also take Randi and Guri with you to prison. I shall go to the sheriff this afternoon and file charges against all of you for arson or accessories to the crime. You shall have until noon to think it over. Your answer will then determine the course I shall take."

"I don't need any time to consider this matter," Marie answered. "My heart has told me long ago that there is no court in the world that can impose on me greater punishment than that of marrying Asle. I will take whatever comes if I should without guilt be sentenced to punishment. I believe, however, that there is such clear evidence of arson that it would be best for the three of us to have the matter come up for trial, but it would be unfortunate for the one who committed the crime."

"Then this is your answer?"

"Yes."

As said, so done. Bonden went to Sheriff

Bye immediately after dinner and demanded that charges be brought against his daughter, and that the other two women be placed in custody.

Chapter Sixteen

The Cotter's Son
In His American Home

Before the trial begins, let us take a trip across the ocean to Ole Haugen. When we left him, he was sick in bed, but now, in the middle of November, we find him much improved. After a week his fever left him, and his feet, which suffered most from the cold, had as a result of the doctor's skill and care healed sufficiently so that he could amble around and do light work for Williams. He hired Ole for one year at a salary of two hundred and forty dollars. The trunk from Carlton arrived together with a letter from Nils Wang and several from Norway. These had reached Carlton shortly after he left and were replies to his second letter.

Williams, always a man to see justice done,

took upon himself the task of bringing suit against Christen Olson, hotel proprietor in Kingston, for refusing lodging for Ole. The proprietor, through Williams' influence, was required to pay twenty-five dollars in doctor bills, six and a half for medicine, twenty dollars for one month's wage, and twenty-three and a half for court costs, a total of seventy-five dollars.

Nellie, the black-haired younger daughter of Williams, was Ole's nurse while he lay convalescing, and Jennie, the elder sister, relieved her off and on at night. The doctor declared that the careful and precise care given Ole contributed a great deal to his rapid recovery. As soon as Ole was better, Nellie enjoyed teaching him to read and write the English language. Williams had promised Ole this instruction for at least two hours every night as long as he desired, and all the books he wanted. Ole progressed rapidly and often engaged in long conversation with the family. One evening when both daughters were in their room, they began talking about him.

"Isn't he a bright boy, Nellie?"

"Yes and what nice blue eyes he has, so full of life, beneath curly locks, and he has such a light and sprightly walk. I never tire of watching him."

"Wonder if his parents in Norway are rich. He surely has had a fine upbringing!"

"No, he told me when he was sick that his parents are poor, and I think the more of him for it. I hope he likes me. He always has a nice smile for me when I pass or stop to talk."

"Yes, but he has that for me too."

"Maybe so, but I am sure he thinks of me twice before he thinks once about you, for I sat up with him twice as much as you when he was sick."

"But, Nellie, don't you think there are other reasons for love than good deeds?"

"Oh, I was not talking about real love. Your thoughts travel too fast for me, my dear Jennie."

"But you meant it anyway."

Meanwhile a similar conversation was going on between their parents. Mr. Williams praised Ole's work and his intelligence and his wife joined in praise of his bravery and courteous manner.

One day when Williams returned from the village he brought two letters from Norway for Ole. Ole opened the letter from Marie first, and as he read his expression changed, as when a dark cloud passes over the sun. Then he read the letter from his parents, apparently it brought no better news, for it told about their eviction from their home. Ole's strong figure went limp and a look of sadness came to his face as he paced the floor. Nellie watched him with great concern, and then ventured to ask him if the letters brought unpleasant news.

"Yes," he replied. "They are making life miserable for my parents and sisters and brother at home, and one of my best friends is accused of crime, although innocent, and has been brought to court by her own father."

"You probably mean your sweetheart?"

"I have never told you that I have a sweetheart as far as I remember," Ole said, blushing.

"No, but I had a feeling that you do, and I saw that one letter was from a woman."

Nellie did not give up before she had a smile on Ole's face, and she began to console herself with the thought that perhaps he did not care so much for her after all. Also, she thought it possible that the letter from his sweetheart, which so depressed him, was notice of the breaking of their engagement.

The Cotter's Son

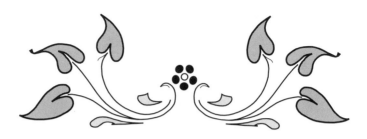

Chapter Seventeen

An Incendiary
Receives His Sentence

Again, let us return to Norway to witness the trial that takes place November the twenty-third. Two of Ole's letters have reached their destination, multiplying the grief of their readers with the news that he had been shamefully cheated and had a most difficult journey from Carlton to Williams' farm. Naturally, the parents had promised their children one thing and another on the strength of their expectations from Ole. They had even gone in debt at one or two business places, promising to pay when this money came. But these worries were overshadowed by their concern for Ole's suffering so far from home.

The leaves on the trees lining the Sigdal

river were gone, traded for layers of snow on the frosty limbs. The countryside was covered with a clean white mantle of snow. Up and down in the valley could be heard a ceaseless rhythm of pounding flails, wielded by cotters on threshing floors, from four o'clock at night. Whack after whack, they separate the grain from straw and chaff. On many farms the worker is required to make four brooms after seven o'clock before he can receive his six shillings for the day's work.

Hovland was dreary and quiet. The cotter was to be ready to take charge of the horses when the officers of the law arrived. Today they came not as visitors; they came to investigate the case against the daughter of the house and two other women. The sheriff and the district judge arrived as Randi Haugen and Guri were talking to Gunhild and Marie in the bedroom. The three who had been on the saeter when the hut was burned were the only ones to be summoned this time. The hearing was held in the parlor.

The complaint stated that on the night of September the fifteenth these three had set fire to the saeter hut belonging to Torsten Hovland. All of them denied the allegation and maintained that it could not have happened through any carelessness on their part, since they did not have a fire after sunset, and the fire that destroyed the building was not detected until long after midnight. Furthermore, it started outside the hut. Also, they testified to the authorities, the morning after the fire they saw footprints outside the house that were not made by a woman but by a large man. Then they presented the key and explained where they found it, and the judge took it for safekeeping. They were asked if they suspected any person of arson and they replied that the only one they could think of was Asle Viig, because they had heard him swear the evening before that he would get vengeance on the women who had offended him. The court made note of the name.

The judge then admonished them to speak the truth only. If they did not, and were found guilty, their punishment would be confinement on bread and water, but if they made full confession their punishment would be much milder. The hearing closed with the announcement that the trial would be held before the court at Lerberg on the tenth of January.

The three accused engaged Attorney Rye,

from Eiker, to defend them. During the Christmas season he came over to Hovland and talked with Marie. He became convinced that Marie and the others were innocent and decided to investigate the case thoroughly.

Marie told him she had found half-burned newspapers here and there around the place. When he asked if she had saved any of these, she recalled that she had wrapped the key that she had found in a piece of newspaper, and that the key was now in the hands of the judge. Rye thereupon went to the judge's home to see the bit of newspaper containing the key, as he had been told. As far as he could make out, the fragment was torn from *Schilling Magazine*, published in Kristiania. On it was an item about a theft in Storgaden, which Rye copied and sent to the publishers with a request that they send him a copy of the paper in which the item was published, together with a list of subscribers receiving the publication at the Sigdal post office. This information was returned to him, revealing that the newspaper copy was dated September 10th, 18--. The names of the subscribers at Sigdal were given as Prost Tandberg and Einar Holst -- no others.

Shortly before the day of the trial, Torsten

Hovland came to the judge and requested him to dismiss the case because it now appeared to be accidental. But the judge replied that Torsten should be old enough to understand that when a criminal case was brought before the court, it could not be lightly dismissed. It must end either by a conviction or a verdict of not guilty.

The day of the trial came and Asle Viig and Einar Holst were also summoned, this time in addition to the three women. Asle was called first, and when questioned he denied all knowledge of the case. He declared that he had never seen the key before, nor had he owned the one on exhibit. He was certain there was not a lock on the Viig farm that the key would open. Supported by several witnesses, he established that he had not been out of the house the night of the fire more than ten minutes at the most.

After this testimony the three accused felt all their hopes vanishing and assumed that their conviction would soon follow. But Torsten Hovland, too, was unhappy. He would gladly have paid a large sum to have kept Marie out of the court, and he certainly never wanted to find Asle involved. He had included his daughter in his charges only to scare her into taking Asle for her betrothed, thinking that at any time he wished he could have the case dismissed.

Einar Holst was called next, and he too denied that he had had any connection with the fire or could give any information at all about it. When asked about the key, he testified that it might be the one he lost on September the seventh, the Sunday night he was with Asle Viig on the saeter.

Although it was not likely that the big key could have been lying where it was found a whole week without being noticed, it was not positive proof that Holst had been there the night before the fifteenth of September. Then Attorney Rye presented a newspaper fragment charred around the edges, and asked if Holst was a subscriber to *Schilling Magazine*. Holst said he had been a subscriber until August, at which time he canceled the subscription. Then the attorney laid the slip of paper before him to prove Holst was on the saeter the night before the fifteenth of September. It was from the publication dated September the tenth and Rye compared the scrap with the complete publication. Since the paper was dated after the seventh of September, and only he and the Prost were subscribers, then it was proof positive that none other than he could have been at the saeter. Later witnesses proved that Holst had been away from Viig for two hours that night, on the pretext that he went to get more playing cards.

After the judge had questioned him on this evidence, Holst at last admitted that he had committed the crime, but refused to give any reason. Because he had known that Guri and Randi were in the hut, and had set the fire outside the door as if to close any means of escape, it was logical to assume that Holst had murder in mind, as it surely would have been if Marie had not arrived and awakened Randi. Holst was placed in irons then and there, by Sheriff Bye, and brought to jail to await trial at the spring session of court.

It was difficult for people to believe that Holst could have committed such a crime, setting fire to property belonging to Torsten Hovland, a man with whom he had never been at odds. Nor could he have had any hatred for Guri or Randi. When the remains from the fire were cleared away Asle's watch was found, a lump of molten metal. So the whole engagement affair came to a very dismal end.

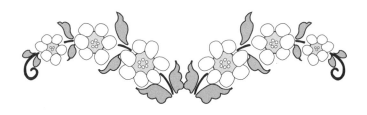

Chapter Eighteen

Bonden's Wife Laid To Rest

Everyone in the valley knew that Torsten Hovland had not managed his farm very well the past several years. He was away too much of the time to give it proper attention, and when he was at home he was intoxicated. He spent more time at the King Carl Hotel in Drammen than at home. There he slept all day, and played cards all night with farmers from Oplandet and cargo-freighters like himself. The stakes often ran into the hundreds of dollars each night. The hotel records showed how much champagne and French cognac he had drunk. He also visited the principal markets in Norway, and always brought with him his famous prize-winning trotters. If anyone passed him on the road, he was ready to buy the faster horse at any price.

Although the farm was free of debt and fertile, with much valuable timberland when he inherited it, Torsten was now over his ears in debt. For many years he had been carrying on a lumber business, but his buying and selling transactions had too often been done at a loss. His wife knew nothing about all this, and he never said a word about business affairs to her. Besides the first loan on the farm, he had incurred a larger short time loan at the Drammen bank in the hope that he could strike a timber deal to raise money, but that failed to come through. Finally an attorney came to Hovland with a protested draft amounting to twelve hundred dollars and said that if it were not made good before sundown the sheriff would be asked to serve an attachment on the place.

When Mother Hovland heard this it became clear to her what she had already felt was impending -- that their financial situation was not as rosy as Torsten had painted it to be.

Torsten thought first that he could gain time by a proffer of brandy, but with no results, for the lawyer was a temperate man. So he was forced to raise the money somewhere else, and he visited several places during the day with no success. The sheriff appeared the next morning and served an attachment on all the horses, cows, and farm machinery. The same week Torsten sold the Hovland timber at a loss to Asle Viig, and with the money he paid the drafts to avoid auctioning off the chattel that had been pledged.

Soon everyone in the valley knew that Torsten Hovland, who a few years before was considered the wealthiest man in the valley, no longer owned his farm. Nevertheless, he continued to live as high as ever, gave many large parties, and took more and more long trips. The days he spent at home he sought the bottle for companionship.

There was little conversation between Torsten and Gunhild. She grew weaker day by day, and seemed to let all earthly matters slip out of her thoughts. Marie was her one joy and interest, to whom she confided that she did not have many days left to live, and that her hour was not far off. She feared that Marie had much to go through alone, when efforts would again be made to force her into a marriage with Asle, and she encouraged Marie to be unyielding to the last, to have confidence that He Who had begun the good work would most assuredly stand by her to the end. She must know that He would not permit weeds to be harvested where He had planted good seed. Even though Gunhild had been in bed since Christmas, Torsten rarely came in to see her. Nor did he seem to have any concern over the outcome of her illness. Her ailment had come on gradually for several years, and Bonden had grown so accustomed to the situation that he thought little about it. It seemed that liquor had petrified his heart, and he was now impervious to tender feelings. Gunhild tried to conceal her sufferings, knowing that Marie suffered with her.

One morning several weeks after the trial, Marie came running to the threshing floor and asked Erick to go over and get Prost Tandberg.

"Mother is so sick," she said. "I don't think she has long to live!"

Prost Tandberg came at once, administered the sacraments, and talked with Gunhild a long time. She was happy to have him with her and was content to meet her fate. Death to her was a relief from a life imposed by her parents, a change to something better. She obtained a promise from Prost Tandberg that in case Marie were mistreated, or if the farm was sold from under them, that he would protect her and, if necessary, let her move to the parsonage.

Shortly after the Prost had arrived, Bonden and Carl Strøm drove up. They went directly into the parlor, talking, laughing, and cursing as loudly as usual, but sobered down in the presence of the Prost. Torsten, however, managed to whisper to Strøm, "It is annoying to have this happen, for I am sure you cannot talk with the girl about such affairs, today, or for many days."

Entering the bedroom Torsten saw at once that Gunhild was much worse, and asked if he might send for a doctor.

"No earthly doctor can help me," whispered Gunhild weakly. "Jesus will heal me. He took the sickness of all of us upon Him. He is with me now, and soon I shall join Him in my heavenly home."

There must have been a soft spot left in Torsten's heart, for when Gunhild asked him if he would sit in with her when she bid farewell to this vale of tears, he answered in a softened tone, "Yes, I will."

Returning to Strøm, Torsten told him that he would have to excuse him for the day, as his wife was dying, and again went back to sit by her side. The Prost had gone, leaving him alone with his wife and daughter.

"Will you make me a promise on my deathbed?" Gunhild said after a pause.

"I will if I can," he replied.

"Will you promise me never again to drink intoxicants?" Gunhild pleaded. "You can still be happy, even if you break with all your drinking friends."

"I dare not," he said, sitting with his head in his hands, deep in thought. It was probably the most honest answer he had ever given her in their twenty years of marriage. "I am afraid I will break the promise."

"But is not your drinking harmful to both body and soul?" she continued. "A year ago I asked a friend to write a letter to you, in the hope that you would pause and reflect on your condition, but he hesitated and said it might be like pouring oil on the fire. However, he wrote these verses which I have been intending to give you, but my courage always failed me. Read them and think about them. Every word is true." Then opening her hymn book she took out a folded piece of paper and handed it to him, which he read in a subdued voice. In simple words, the poem painted the ruinous effects of indulgence in liquor, and pleaded earnestly with him to stop the habit.

Torsten folded the paper, put it in his pocket, and sat in deep thought again, silent and immovable as a statue.

Gunhild's parents, the Lie folks, now entered the room and greeted her in whispered words and inquired about her condition.

"I am happier now to begin my last journey than I was when I obeyed your wishes and against my will came to this house. You did it to better my temporal welfare, but forgot my spiritual happiness. Your kind intentions have not been realized. However, you have always had my forgiveness. May God forgive you, and may we meet again."

As her parents were leaving there came through the door a pale woman, simply dressed, and Gunhild's face brightened as she recognized Randi Haugen. She was already too weak to talk much, but she and Randi communed heart to heart, in a language their eyes could speak so well.

"I saw the Prost come over here," Randi said at last. "I thought from this that you were not well, and I knew I would have no peace until I went over and talked with you, but maybe Torsten doesn't want me to be here." She glanced at Bonden, who continued to sit motionless by the window.

"Never mind," said Gunhild. "How are the folks at Svartbraaten?"

"Oh, we can't complain," said Randi, "but it hurts me every time I see Haugen cottage. I seem to see Ole also, and so many memories come to mind. The little plots of soil between the rocks which we worked so carefully for twenty years became as dear to us as if they were our own. God knows it was hard to leave the place, in spite of the fact that it produced more sweat than gain."

Gunhild looked at Torsten again and said, "Since you could not grant my first request, will you agree to this one, that for my sake you return the Haugen place to Torkil and Randi, and draw up a contract to the effect that they shall have it for the rest of their lives?"

Gunhild looked at Torsten again and said, "That I shall do. I will send Erick over with a horse to move them back today, if they so wish. I acknowledge that I acted in haste and should not have driven them away from the place."

Randi looked joyfully over to Gunhild,

while she thanked God that he had heard her prayer and so moved her husband's heart that she could not see more honesty in him than at any time before. A long silence followed, with Bonden sitting silent as before. Then Gunhild took Marie's hand and said to her, "I have a secret concerning you, my child, but the time has not yet come to reveal it. Do not use force -- prayer and faith will bring victory to you, even before the battle is over."

She asked Marie to sing the hymn, *Jesus, Your Sweet Union Attain,* and as she began to sing, the Lie folks came into the room and joined Marie and Randi Haugen in the singing. A look of peace came over Gunhild as the hymn ended, and she turned her eyes upon each one of the group before her and whispered, "Yes, God is good. He has brought you here to my bedside for my last hour. There are two whom I miss, yet I know for certain that they will be with us in heaven."

These were her last words. All was quiet.

Torsten paced back and forth, looking at his wife as if he wanted to say, "I had so many things I would have liked to talk to you about -- to confess and to share with you, but time was so short."

He left the room, fighting back tears but too proud to let anyone see his grief. His heart was softened, though only a little.

Marie wept bitterly and whispered to Randi, "Mother is no more, will you take her place?"

Randi took her hand and answered, "As long as I live, you shall not need to call yourself motherless. I am poor and have little room in my house, but I have much room in my heart."

The following Sunday was a clear, sunny day. At Hovland spruce cuttings set in the snow lined both sides of the driveway from the house to the main road. The yard in front of the house was filled with horses and sleighs, and from the parlor came the sounds of hymn singing. Six men came through the door carrying a coffin completely covered with flowers, which they placed upon a long sleigh, to which a black horse was hitched. Men and women dressed in black followed the coffin. Women were drying tears with white handkerchiefs. Soon the sleighs began to move, and the procession headed southward to the Holum church, where bells were tolling their message: "Time is passing -- bells are ringing -- all must -- pass this way --

repent -- come ye here and find peace."

The women went into the house, except for two who remained standing on the steps and watched the funeral procession disappear. One was a pale, elderly woman with a cast of sadness on a good and kindly face. The other was a tall, beautiful girl, whose fairness was accentuated by black clothing. The young woman was weeping unrestrainedly, and turning to her companion she said, "Now, I understand the meaning of the saying, 'What is home without a mother?'"

Poor people who met the procession broke twigs off the spruce trees and from the side of the road tossed them in front of the funeral sleigh. They had heard that it was good, kindhearted and helpful Mother Hovland that today was being brought to her last resting place.

Then, as the coffin was about to be lowered into the grave, there appeared a stranger among the mourners. He walked up to the coffin and asked that if be opened so that he might place a wreath on the breast of the dead woman. He was Peder Olsen, also known as Halte-Per (Limping Pete), who lived alone in a hut far over the ridge. He was a shy man, and now folks assumed that he was mentally deranged, for nothing more was known about his relations with the deceased than that Peder had served at Lie a few years. His request was refused, so he laid the simple wreath on the cover. A ring was tied to the wreath, bystanders noticed, and a closer examination would have revealed an inscription -- "Peder Olsen" and the stamp "Genuine." After pausing a moment with his hat over his heart, Peder limped away as the coffin, with the wreath on it, was lowered into the grave.

Chapter Nineteen

The Cotters Return
To Their Old Home

The Haugen folks moved back to their old
home the day after Gunhild's death. They
had nearly everything they needed now, for
both had worked for Lie in the fall and
Torkil had chopped wood during the winter,
and so had earned more than they could
have done at Hovland. At any rate they
returned to Haugen in a far happier mood
than when they went away, but the loss of
the good lady at Hovland was of far more
consequence to them than many realized.
Marie was glad to have them back. She spent
many evenings with them in the winter and
she felt that the loss of her mother would
have been unbearable if she had not had the
Haugen folks to share her grief and problems.

Torkil resumed his work at Hovland after Bonden had drawn up a new and better contract, keeping his promise to his wife on her deathbed. Bonden did not give any large parties after Gunhild died, and Marie cherished the hope that a change might take place within him. But soon he rejoined his old friends and sought to drown his sorrows in the liquor. He had no timber to sell that winter and often needed money, still he continued the old pattern of riotous living.

As far as Marie was concerned, he soon learned that he could not sell her to Asle. He concluded that she must be engaged to the cotter's son because she had turned away any and all who came to Hovland. His suspicion was strengthened by information he received from the postmaster that Torkil Haugen at various times had mailed letters to Ole, and that there was a letter for Marie whenever Torkil received one from America. Torsten asked the postmaster to send word to him the next time there was a letter for Marie, so that he might bring it to her himself.

Chapter Twenty

A Horrifying Experience On The Prairie

Again spring had come to the prairie. In Norway, court had been held in Lerberg, and Holst received a sentence of nine years in prison, which would be reduced to seven if he revealed the reason for the arson attempt and if there were any others involved.

On the Williams farm in Wisconsin, Ole Haugen was sitting in his room one Sunday writing letters. He appeared in a happy mood, for before him lay a money order for sixty dollars to the Norwegian Credit Bank in Kristiania. He had received two letters the month before with news of his parents' return to Haugen and Mother Hovland's death. The one letter cheered him, but the other could not have grieved him more. He answered both letters and enclosed the sixty dollars to his parents.

He had worked nearly six months for Mr. Williams, who often said to his neighbors that the contract was for one year but he wished that it were for ten. He noticed that Nellie and Ole liked each other and it became the accepted fact among the few farmers in the neighborhood that Nellie would marry the Norseman.

Ole counted the days required to get a return letter, so he could be sure that his letters reached home safely. He knew how happy Marie would be each time she read his letters and the joy the letter containing more money would bring to his parents. He pictured to himself what they would say when they found themselves possessors of sixty dollars. As these thoughts passed through his mind he could work with enthusiasm. Nellie was delighted that Ole was in such a particularly happy frame of mind, for she considered herself partly responsible and as her hopes grew, so did her display of affection. The little black-haired girl that everyone called the "Prairie Beauty" really loved Ole, and nursed a hope of requited love, letting her feelings be known at times.

A couple of months after mailing his letters, Ole began to make frequent inquiries for mail at the post office in Kingston, but no letters arrived for him. He called often at the post office during the next two months, but when he read news about shipwrecks he concluded that his letters were lost. With this in mind that the letters had not reached them he wrote again to Marie and his parents.

Long before the end of the year, Williams and Ole reached an agreement for the following year, this time for three hundred dollars. About six miles from his farm lay a quarter section of land where Williams had broken up a few acres. He advised Ole to take a homestead on this land, and Ole agreed. Williams helped later in building a house and making other improvements. When Ole returned from the claim, Williams would tell Nellie how nicely things were coming on "her farm," as he called it. Nellie would smile with satisfaction. Ole may have done the same, but Norway would come to his mind again. It was late in the fall, and no answer had come to his first letters or to the later ones. He became downhearted, complaining often in the presence of the family. They, too, could not imagine the cause of the delay.

Although Nellie did not like to see Ole so unhappy, she was not displeased to think that perhaps now his sweetheart had forgotten him. Ole began to suspect that Marie's letters might have been pilfered by someone or another. He suspected her father particularly, but what of his parents' letters? Could it be that both were dead? However, if that were so, someone would have written to him about it. Such were the thoughts passing through his mind when he wrote to Sexton Aas and asked him kindly to inform him of the reason for the delay of his letters. He asked if he could let him know within a couple of months. Christmas came and was gone, another two months passed, and still no letters. Not even one from Sexton Aas. It seemed to Ole that the postal service between America and Norway had broken down completely, and his despair became greater than his friend Nellie could understand.

At last, in the spring, he decided to write to the bank in Kristiania to find out if the money order he sent had been cashed there.

It was now time for him to go over to the claim and live there for a period to fulfill the requirement of the law regarding homesteads.

With Williams' help he got together a little oven, some kitchen utensils and food, placed them on the sleigh, and left in high spirits for the little cabin. There they brought the oven in, started a fire, and made coffee. Though it was just eleven o'clock they sat down to eat the noon meal.

"This will be the first meal ever served in this house," Williams said.

"Yes, and it would be interesting to know when I shall eat my last meal here," answered Ole.

"When you get married, I presume."

"I don't think so."

"Oh, I think it's best that you bring Nellie over here to take care of the house for you until fall when you move over here, for you cannot very well be alone."

"That's a nice offer, but I don't believe she would be satisfied with working for a poor Norseman in a little hut like this, nor do I believe her parents willing to place her on such a job either."

"But I believe a lifetime contract could easily be arranged, regardless of nationality and the house," Williams said in a rather determined tone. "And as far as her parents are concerned, I never say 'No' to a good prospect, for the future looks brighter for you than for most young men. You are an industrious and intelligent worker, and you'll never want for bread, though you should remain a laborer. However, you have good judgment, and I do not flatter you. My advice is to cultivate your land, then sell it at a profit. Then take the profits and go into some business, for that is what you are well-suited for."

A long silence followed, and Ole began to wonder how he could forget his dear ones in Norway, if he should learn that death was the reason he had not heard from them for so long. He knew that it would be a great shock to receive word that Marie had died. Such an event would greatly change his plans. "Should my parents also be dead," he thought, "then the wisest thing would be to bring my brother and sisters over here, then marry Nellie, for she has so many good qualities beside her beauty that one could not help but love her, and what a bright future for the children! What a pleasure to have Nellie to teach them the language too. But could I with clear conscience marry her if Marie is dead? I have done all I could to find out about the situation, and would probably never have to condemn myself for having broken faith with Marie. For who would remain unmarried all through life because his sweetheart had died?"

"Marie would," came a whispered thought in his ear.

His day dreaming was interrupted by Williams, who arose from the table and started to hang pictures on the walls -- pictures that Nellie had sent along.

Nothing more was said, and Williams prepared to go home, while Ole set out for Kingston, four miles away from the claim. It was his intention to buy string and make a fishing net during the days he stayed at the claim, to present to Williams, and therefore he kept his trip to town a secret from Williams.

It was a beautiful day when he set out at noon, but before he reached town the sky had clouded over and it turned dark as before a storm. A mild south wind that had been blowing suddenly veered to the northwest, and fifteen minutes after he reached Kingston the drifting snow was so dense that it was hard to see across the street. But without heeding the merchant's insistent advice, Ole started homeward. His land was northwest from town, so he had the wind directly in his face. He lost track of the road after he left town, but thought he could reach the woods surrounding his house by keeping on directly against the wind. He could barely see five feet ahead of him and the mixture of snow and sleet cut him in the face, so that it was difficult to keep his eyes open. Then he began to regret that he had not taken the merchant's advice and turned in the opposite direction, following the wind to Kingston. He walked and walked, and began to wonder why it took longer to get back to town than it had coming from it. But soon the riddle was solved -- a changing wind had led him to strange places on the level prairie. It began to get dark, the storm raged more furiously than ever, and the temperature dropped rapidly. He became desperate, and began to wonder if he could save his life. Then a vision of Marie came to him and she scolded him for leaving her to go to this strange land only to die on the prairie and be eaten by wild animals. Better that he should rest by her side in mother earth at Holum church. He felt now that Marie would always be clos-est to his heart and he was happy at this dis-covery. At the same time he could not escape blaming himself for ever thinking of forgetting Marie, for were not his very last words to Marie if death should tear her from him:

God's Will be done, now I must go,
In Heaven shall our wedding be.

He had in his thoughts sought escape from these words and could not now die with good conscience.

Rescue seemed more and more impossible. He neither said nor heard anything but the whine of the wind as he began to feel sleepy and weary from his struggle. Suddenly, the sound of a dog's bark caught his ear, but it disappeared as quickly. He stopped and listened, wondering if it was Rover, William's dog. He was cheered by the hope that now he was near the farm, and he started in the direction of the sound. After a few minutes he saw Rover right before him. The dog jumped and sprang about and appeared overjoyed to have found Ole. He started to the left, returned, tugged at Ole's overcoat to hurry him on. Ole followed, feeling assured that the dog knew the direction to take better than he did.

When they came to a swamp overgrown with rank grass, the dog began to whine mournfully and dig the snow away with his forepaws, at what Ole surmised was a hummock and a hiding place for a wild animal. After failing to call the dog away, he finally went over to see what it was. The hummock turned out to be two women, undoubtedly Nellie and Jennie Williams, though it was hard to recognize them at first in the darkness. They were lying side by side, hand in hand with their faces towards the ground. Their hands were apparently frozen, but their heavy coats had still kept some warmth in their unconscious bodies. Prompt action was necessary, for they could not be left a moment longer. If they could be brought home they might possibly be revived, for they could not have been lying there very long, Ole thought.

One hope remained. If they were not far from the farm, Rover could lead them. Tired but determined, Ole summoned almost super-human strength, with the one thought that if something were to be done it must be done now. Lifting the girls from the snow and carrying one under each arm, he followed the dog that ran ahead barking with joy, but no faster than Ole could follow him.

He had struggled about a half a mile through the deep snow when his arms could hold their burden no longer, and he had to

The Cotter's Son

lay them down on the snow and rest.

He looked around, but saw no light. The snow was falling so fast that when he looked down he saw the two girls were already covered with snow. His courage wavered, but he thought, "I shall die if I lie down. Why not struggle to the last and die that way?"

His heavy clothes handicapped him, so he removed his overcoat and threw it down, mumbling to himself, "I can quickly earn a coat if I can save my life." He lifted the two girls out of the snow, and again carried one under each arm, following the dog who pulled his coat in an attempt to drag it with him.

Another half mile behind him and again Ole stopped for rest. As he laid down his burden he heard some wild animal, perhaps a rabbit, run out of hiding, and the dog, following his natural instincts, dropped the coat and followed the animal. Not wishing to lose his guide, Ole tried to call the dog and discovered then that he had lost his voice. The dog was gone, and no light was to be seen, making it almost hopeless to think of saving himself. Ole sat down exhausted in the deep snow, soaked with perspiration, his friends on each side of him. Drops rolled down his cheeks and froze into ice before they reached his chin. He felt the unrelenting cold wind cut straight through him. Jumping up, he discovered that one of his arms was not able to lift its burden. Should he try to take one with him or should he give up?

Jennie had no overshoes, and her feet were as hard as stone. Ole took the coat that the dog had been dragging, wrapped her feet with it, and tied it on with his handerchief, then took Nellie under his arm. He reasoned that if by help of the wind he could keep the course that the dog had led them on, he might save one of the sisters at least, with himself -- better than letting them all die. If he reached the Williams house, someone could go back to try to find Jennie. But he had not taken many steps before he felt compelled to look back and the sight of the helpless being stretched out on the snow, left to a certain death -- if she were not already dead -- was more than he could stand. So he laid Nellie down and went back for Jennie, carried her as far past Nellie as he still was able to see Nellie behind him. By doing this he gained a quarter of a mile, and then to his great joy he saw a light and knew that he was near Williams' house. "If I could be sure that I could find the way back to this place, I would go on with one, and someone could go back with me and find the other," he reasoned. "This way I have to travel the road twice." Then remembering the two large balls of strong twine he had with him, he tied one end to Jennie's arm. Then he let the twine unwind from the ball in his pocket as he pushed forward towards the light, with Nellie in his arms. His heart was pounding in his breast when he reached the garden gate and recognized the place. Then summoning his last ounce of strength, he again struggled forward, but before he reached the house he felt a peculiar sensation, as if he were fainting. Fear came over him, for he realized that in a storm like this twenty feet from the house could be as certain death as twenty miles. He staggered yet a few more feet, and then fell with his burden into the arms of Mrs. Williams.

Now he was on the Atlantic Ocean on the homeward journey to Norway, with calm sea and pleasant weather. The ship rocked like the cradle at Hovland, and he saw the coast of Norway. The ship laid to at the side of a high mountain, and he tried in vain to find the reason for landing here where they could not get ashore. He felt himself carried by unseen hands high up to the peak of the mountain, where he could see unending plains ahead. Out in the middle of the plain stood a tall beacon that shone brighter than the sun. He started to walk in the direction of the light, with a basketful of roses which he brought from America for Marie. When he reached shore the beacon vanished, and in its place stood Marie, so brightly beautiful and her hair shining like gold. Soon he was with her, took her hand in his, and received a smile that had never seemed so sweet. But she said nothing. He continued walking, and she took the basket and followed him. He asked how things were at Hovland, and in a voice that seemed to come from heaven, she answered, "Rose bushes, flowers, birches, brooks, and birds are unchanged; but every-thing built by the hands of man -- all of that is destroyed. But what of it! We shall play and sing, live and be glad as the birds, and that is all we need, for the garden shall be our home for eternity."

As they walked along, Ole noticed that the roses in the basket had become the most beautiful wreath that he had ever seen. They set the basket down, their eyes met, and again the same dazzlingly sweet smile greeted him, while he took the garland of roses and placed it on her head.

Now he awoke. Someone touched his pillow. He looked around and it seemed to him that room and contents were familiar. So also was the man that stood before him. In his confusion, he asked in a hoarse voice, "Am I in Norway or America?"

"You are in America. In your own room in the good old home of Mr. Williams," Dr. Jones answered, for it was he that stood before him with bottle and spoon in his hands.

As soon as Mr. and Mrs. Williams learned that Ole was awake, they came in from their daughters' rooms and began to heap upon him their gratitude. They told him that their daughters were alive, both had high fever, but there was still hope for them.

Ole also had a fever and took the medicine the doctor gave him. Later, Mrs. Williams sat down on the side of his bed and said, "It's two o'clock at night now. Never in my life have I spent twelve hours such as these last have been, so filled with dread and apprehension and frightful experiences, now we gratefully rejoice that they are over, as you must do, too. It was about midday yesterday, when the weather was fine, that Nellie and Jennie went over to Smith's for a short visit. In the afternoon it commenced to storm, as you know. We did not think they had started on the way home, although we felt uneasy about it, but what could we do? We could only hope until you stumbled in with Nellie in your arms -- certainly she had wished to be yours but never could she have been more so than now, if she is spared to live. Then as our joy and fear calmed down, we noticed the twine unraveled from the ball in your pocket leading out through the door. Then we knew that it was your device for saving Jennie, but you had fainted and could not tell us. We followed the twine along the garden fence in the black, stormy night and just beyond the garden the line seemed to be fastened to the ground. But by brushing aside the snow and following the line, to our amazement we found it tied to Jennie's arm. She was covered so completely with snow that without the line she could not have been found before the snow melted. We carried her home, bathed her in cold water as we had bathed Nellie and in a short time the doctor arrived."

When Mrs. Williams finished telling about Jennie's rescue, Mr. Williams told how Dr. Jones had arrived quickly in spite of the terrible night. The doctor owned a farm by the river about two miles from Williams, and was living there. Williams took two horses, riding one and leading the other, and following the edge of the woods, all the way in ten minutes he knocked at the doctor's door -- as if he would knock the house to pieces. The doctor ran to the door, revolver in hand, as Williams gasped out, "Dress quickly and follow me and save three lives, if possible.

"Take that horse and don't spare its life, for it's a question of saving human life!" Williams cried out to him. Seven or eight minutes later the unconscious victims of the storm were under the doctor's care.

"Nothing less than an unbelievable feat is what Ole has done in saving two others with himself in this wild prairie storm, when an ordinary person could not even save himself," exclaimed Mrs. Williams.

"It takes a man like Ole to do that sort of thing," Williams added and the doctor declared that such heroism deserved renown and honor all over America.

The doctor remained in the house through

the week, and before his departure Ole was able to get on his feet. The girls lavished their thanks on him for his superhuman efforts to save them from certain death.

"After God, I am happy to accept your thanks," Ole replied, while Nellie hugged him warmly.

Jennie could only reach out her hand to him. She was unable to raise herself, and a week later she went to sleep never to waken. Her death was a grievous loss for the parents and sister to bear, but the tragedy could not compare with what it would have been if the parents had found their daughters both dead out on the hummock in the swamp.

Nellie recovered, and was drawn to Ole more than ever. Neighbors and her family assumed that they should one day marry, and as Ole received no letter from Norway Nellie felt certain that she would win him. He regarded her more fondly than before, so that the parents did not doubt that he was in love with her. Still, Nellie could not understand why Ole never openly revealed his love for her.

About a week after that stormy night, Ole read in several newspapers a detailed account of the incident on the prairie, in which he was praised as a great hero and was referred to as Williams' future son-in-law.

Five weeks passed without anything of note, but then Ole received an answer from the Norwegian credit bank, stating that the draft had been paid the twenty-third of May the previous year. This convinced him that the letters had arrived at the Sigdal post office, and that there they had fallen into the hands of someone other than his parents or Marie. Without delay he sent the following registered letter to:

Sheriff Bye
Sigdal P.O.
via Drammen, Norway:
   In the first part of May last year, I sent to my father, Torkil O. Haugen, sixty dollars by draft to the Norwegian Credit Bank, Kristiania, but failed to hear from him, although I wrote to him again last August. Early in November, I wrote to Sexton Aas requesting him to inform me if my parents were living and if they had received the money, but here I was again disappointed in my expectations to receive an answer. This spring I wrote to the bank, and I just received the reply that the draft was cashed the twenty-third of May last year, which proves that someone, if not my

father, has received the letter.

I have also had correspondence with Marie T. Hovland. In view of the fact that I have always been a thorn in the flesh to her father, it may therefore be suspected that Torsten Hovland has destroyed our correspondence in one way or another, so that they would consider me dead, for I have not heard from anyone for more than a year. It might also be that Torsten kept the money intended for my father, and I ask you kindly to investigate the case.

If you should find Torsten Hovland or any other one guilty of wrong doing in connection with this matter, I wish nevertheless that no one be arrested unless necessary for the prosecution of the case.

Respectfully,

Ole T. Haugen

Chapter Twenty-One

Bonden A Criminal

One morning late in May several travelers were sitting in the parlor at Hovland reading newspapers. Torsten had been reading *Morgenbladet*, but rose quickly and went into the living room, where Marie was sitting at her sewing table. Pointing to an article in the newspaper he said, "Read this about your old sweetheart and see how you have been taken in."

Marie took the paper and read:

"American newspapers tell about a Norseman by the name of Ole T. Haugen, who has worked during the last year and a half for a Yankee, Charles Williams, in Wisconsin. He has revealed heroism and presence of mind by saving the lives of Williams' two daughters from certain death out on the prairie during a stormy night last winter. One of these is described as the "Belle of the Prairie" and the Norseman has the honor of calling her his sweetheart and will shortly become her husband."

She read the piece but could not believe her eyes. She read it over again, and then the meaning became clear. Name and place corresponded, so the hero could not be any other than Ole. The grief and anxiety she had gone through the past winter because of failure to receive letters from Ole, had left her uncertain whether he was alive or dead, but all this did not compare with the shock she received from the newspaper article. Had Ole, too, deceived her? He who had been as faithful and unchangeable as the Sigdal mountain -- clean and transparent as the mountain stream! For him she would give her life, and if he were dead she would live out her life alone!

She put the paper away and went up to her room, brought a photograph of Ole out of its hiding place, and looked at it intently. "So Ole is going to marry that American girl?" she thought wildly. "No, now I do not believe it! Such a thing is impossible! The story in *Morgenbladet* is not true."

Then in her confusion and dismay she thought she heard a voice whispering in her ear, telling her to be calm, that Ole lived, and lived only for her! Three sleepless nights passed and she hovered between hope and despair. On the fourth day, looking out the living room window, she was startled to see Sheriff Bye and Merchant Borg driving up to the house and Randi and Torkil Haugen walking behind them.

"Unhappy folks," she thought. "Has something happened again involving them with this sheriff?"

Bonden met them on the front steps and all went into the parlor. Marie listened and heard them speak of the weather as customary, and then the sheriff asked her father why he had not forwarded the letters which he had received from the post office for Torkil Haugen. Torsten answered, "I do not recall that I have received any letters that I have not delivered to the addressee, but if that has happened it must have been an oversight."

"May I prod your memory," the sheriff went on. "These poor folks have not received mail from their son in America for a year and a half, and Merchant Berg, standing there, can testify to the fact that at least two letters were received from him last spring and summer, and that they were sent with you when you called for the mail. With each letter for the parents, there was one for Marie also. Have you delivered these to her?"

"Ye - es . . . I must have done so -- I can't remember for sure," Torsten said hesitatingly.

Marie was then called in by the sheriff, who asked her, "Have you received two letters from Ole T. Haugen, now in America, since last spring?"

"No, I have not received a letter from him for over a year and a half, and I have come to believe that he is dead," Marie responded.

"Well, Torsten Hovland, now comes the big and important question," Sheriff Bye continued. "Why did you not deliver the draft for sixty dollars written in favor of its rightful owner, instead of forging his name and collecting the money for yourself? If you were clever and brazen enough to take the money from these poor folks, you should have known that you could not get away with it later."

"Draft? Money! I don't understand what you are talking about," Torsten sputtered and tried to laugh off the whole matter.

"Well, it is immaterial whether you

remember or not, for we have all the facts
regarding what happened, and such clear
proof that we do not need any more evidence," answered the sheriff as he displayed
legal-looking papers that he held in his hand.
"Before you are Postmaster Berg, and Torkil
and his wife, and here is a letter from Ole
Haugen requesting investigation of the case."
He then read the letter, omitting the last
part. "And look, here is your own letter, in
your handwriting, that you sent to the bank
in which you have used Torkil Haugen's
name. I have borrowed it for further proof of
forgery. In Berg's post office records we found
your signature on the receipt of payment for
the draft drawn in favor of Torkil for sixty
dollars, only eight days before the date of
your letter. To obtain this from the post
office you forged an order using Torkil's
name. Of these dealings Torkil and his wife
know absolutely nothing. Now, what more
proof is necessary?"

Torsten stood silent and pondered awhile,
then answered: "I have quite forgotten these
matters and had laid them aside, but it has
all been done with the good intention of
turning the money over to him from the
draft, for as you know, he cannot write. You

must know that I have so much to take care of, and so many lines of business, that I cannot remember everything. But if the situation is as you say, he shall have his money. I did not mean to cheat him. I shall go directly to Viig. I have some business to do with Asle and shall get the money from him, for there is not enough in my account."

"You shall not leave the house!" the sheriff said firmly, and rattled handcuffs which he held in his hand. "You are now my prisoner, and we have not finished with you yet. You have opened and stolen so many letters that you likely will never be a free man again. I have, however, orders to go easy with you if you confess and explain all you did. We can send word to Asle Viig if you wish."

Erick was sent over to Viig for the money, and meanwhile Bonden confessed that he committed the frauds in order to get Marie to believe the Ole was dead or had forgotten her. To accomplish this, he had to prevent Torkil from receiving his letters. He had read Marie's letters, and confessed that their warm, frank, and unselfish contents moved him almost to the point of giving up the plan and letting the correspondence go on, but the evil forces in him became master and the let-

The Cotter's Son

ter remained in his pocket. He thought that there was something nice about the letters to Torkil too, showing that the son was trying to pay something on the old family debt. But since he was pressed for money, the temptation was too great and he decided to use the draft for himself. He confessed also that another person in the valley was involved in the affair with the letters, who had promised to help if anything was discovered.

"Furthermore," continued the sheriff, "you also opened the mail bags when you carried the mail, for Berg remembers that at different times the previous summer letters were mailed to Ole Haugen, and Ole has written that he never received a one."

"No, I never opened the mailbags," Torsten answered, "for I could not get hold of a key that fit, but I asked the postmaster at Sand to return the letters because the senders had asked to get them back because the addresses were wrong. I also took the letter addressed to Klokker Aas, reasoning that since it came from America it must be from Ole and that there might be questions about the other letters and the money, so that I did not dare to let it be delivered."

Erick now returned with the money in hand and gave it to Torsten. The sheriff commanded him to give sixty-four dollars and twenty-four shillings to Torkil, as he figured seven percent on the capital as interest for one year. Bonden complied promptly, and used none of the abusive language he was in the habit of using when a shilling had to be paid to the cotter. Torkil shook when he received the money -- he had never been so rich. Randy rocked her head from side to side and thought about her son, and surely Marie's thoughts were the same.

"Did you burn all the letters?" the sheriff questioned further.

"No, I often stood before the fire ready to throw them in, but there was always something holding me back. I was afraid to carry them in my pocket. They are hidden in the cellar, in the northwest corner."

The package was found, containing fourteen letters -- five from Ole to his parents and three to Marie, six were addressed to Ole, of which three were from his parents and three from Marie, the last being unopened.

When the sheriff returned from the cellar with the missing letters in his hand, he said,

"You have a bad case on your hands, Torsten, one that could put you in company with Holst at Akerhus prison. You can be glad that the people involved are willing to forgive, mostly because of your daughter. I demand that you apologize to Torkil and Randi, also to Marie and ask their forgiveness. Then I have the authority to give you your freedom, inasmuch as you have confessed everything."

Bonden went over to Marie who was weeping quietly, with her eyes on the bundle of letters. He took her by the hand, at the same time covering his face with his handkerchief. Then, he asked forgiveness from the others. Sheriff Bye opened the pack of letters, give Marie and Torkil theirs, and kept the six for Ole to be forwarded with a letter from himself. This met with the approval of everyone.

Chapter Twenty-Two

A Settlement
Between Ole And Nellie

About the same time as Bonden's pilfering of the mail was discovered, Ole and Nellie were driving to the church in Kingston one Sunday. Ole was dressed in a new suit, so it was not surprising that Mrs. Williams should remark to her husband as they stood in the kitchen door looking at them, "They will make a fine couple, Ole and Nellie."

When they had gone some distance down the road, Ole slowed the horse to a walk. "I have a weighty matter on my heart that I should have talked over with you a long time ago, my dear Nellie," he began. "I have noticed your feelings for me, warmer than just friendship, and I realize that they go beyond any worth of mine or appreciation of

The Cotter's Son

services to you. In one way I am very pleased, but on the other hand it troubles me very much."

He looked at her, and she blushed and said, "Are you troubled because I love you? Have you then no such feelings to return?"

"Yes," replied Ole, "It's just because I think so much of you that I am troubled. I love you more than I have a right to!"

"But should it be necessary to ask permission to love anyone you hold dear?"

"Yes, in many situations, and especially in mine, for I must frankly confess to you that my heart was given away long before I saw this country, or you. I feel that I have made unworthy use of that which belongs to another, when I have indulged in love for you after first swearing faithfulness to another."

"But she has not written to you for over a year. Can you continue to rely on her love or think yourself under obligation to her?"

"Oh, yes!" Ole protested. "We have known each other as far back as our memories reach. Ten years would not be enough to dim the glow or weaken the confidence between us, and I have unshakable confidence in her faithfulness. I am certain that she is either dead, or our mail has been tampered with or stolen by someone who wishes to separate us."

"If she should be dead, what then?"

"I hope that is not so, but if it were, then I am still under the same pledge. I have therefore no right to love any other one."

Nellie began to weep and said nothing for a long time. At last she said, "Before we started talking I sat here happy in the thought that it would not be long before I would drive this road to church with you to bind the tie that I have dreamed of for a whole year, but now in a few minutes the lovely dream is gone forever. It took only a few minutes to ruin the house I have been building for a year. If you do not have the right to love anyone but your sweetheart in Norway, by the same token I do not have the right to love anyone but you, for I owe my existence to you. You are so much a part of my heart that it would be death to me to destroy that love suddenly. I could now be tempted to cry out, 'Why did you not let me lie out there on the edge of the swamp where you found me, or why did you not carry Jennie home first, and leave me to catch the deadly fever, instead of saving my life only to plunge me into grief and pain?'"

They had now reached Kingston, and the conversation was not resumed when they were returning home. But Nellie's eyes were red with weeping when they arrived at the farm.

Nellie's parents were told of the situation, and although they deeply regretted it, both for themselves and even more because of their daughter, to their credit it may be said that they never tried to talk Ole into breaking his troth with Marie. On the contrary, they admired him for his steadfastness. They recognized in him a character more admirable than was commonly found. As for Ole and Nellie, they pledged an agreement that mutual friendship should always exist between them.

Chapter Twenty-Three

Ole Writes To Marie

When Ole came down for breakfast one morning, the family noted that he was unusually sober and thoughtful. He told them he had so peculiar a dream that he could hardly say it was just a dream. He went to work right after breakfast while Williams went into town. When he returned he gave Ole three letters and a thick bundle containing seven more letters from Norway.

"Well, now you have all the news in one big lump," said Williams. But Ole was too preoccupied with the letters to hear a word he might have said to him.

The letters all brought good news from those who for so long a time had considered him dead. Sheriff Bye gave him complete information about how Torsten Hovland chose to confess and how the money was paid to his parents with interest. He filled in all the details about finding the letters in the cellar and delivering them to the proper recipients and included a reply from Klokker Aas. Marie complained that it hurt her so to read in *Morgenbladet* that he was to be married to Williams' daughter, and at first she thought that this was the reason why he did not write, but she could never make herself believe that this was true. Then Sheriff Bye came to her after a few days and cleared up the whole case relating to the letters. As for their engagement, she would take Ole's word when he himself wrote it. Ole now understood the interpretation of his dream, and wrote the following letter:

Dear Marie:

Through the mail today I received so many precious letters that I know the power of the pen to be greater than I ever imagined. Yet it cannot convey my feelings when I opened and read the letters from you and learned of events of the past year and a half. That a father could have the heart to inflict such grief on his daughter and believe such action to be for her own good is something that passes my understanding.

Concerning Nellie Williams, I believe I can best explain by telling you a dream I had last night:

As I walked along a country road I saw three fields which had been plowed and planted. In the first the good soil was shallow and the plants withered and dried. The second was better but was choked with weeds and the plants were stunted. The third field had vigorously growing plants to the very edges and bore perfectly ripened fruit. The plants were cared for from the beginning and their roots could withstand any storm. Later attempts to put in plants between the large ones had failed.

This dream resembles the parable of the sower, but it also tells a story of love. How two people can fall suddenly in love, but like a flower it will be of short duration. And how often have we not seen love develop like a plant rooted in rich soil until difficulties of all sorts like weeds smother their early feelings of affection? But my love for you is different. The field in my dream was planted to the edges just as my heart is filled only with you. The plants were well-cared from the beginning, just as we were from childhood through the years, so that even at the edge of confirmation our love was so firmly fixed that it could not be uprooted by the storm your father raised, or wilt-

ed because I was lost to you for awhile. Attempts to plant between us soon faded away.

Does not this closely parallel my friendship with Nellie? I confess a love for her because she is a fine person and has done a great deal for me, but at the same time it is not the kind of love I have for you. The dream revealed that your love crowded out affection for anyone else. Be therefore assured that whatever happens, I am the same faithful and devoted.

Ole

P.S. Next Sunday I shall write a longer letter to you telling about my situation now.
Best wishes!

Chapter Twenty-Four

Ole In Chicago

Throughout the summer and fall, Ole had regular correspondence with Marie, and no one ventured to come between them. Toward fall he received an offer of ten dollars per acre for his claim, and did not delay selling the one hundred and sixty acres for sixteen hundred dollars. He read in the newspaper that Chicago was booming, and real estate was doubling, and he was tempted to go there and try his luck when his year with Williams ended. His plan was first to get a job. He arrived in Chicago with the nineteen hundred dollars he had earned and saved, and for which he knew he was indebted to Charles Williams. Eighteen hundred he put in the bank and seventy-five he sent to his parents.

It was easy to get a job in Chicago that fall. Ole found employment in one of the large mills on the north side, with good pay. His employers soon discovered that he was a good worker and promoted him first to night watchman and later to shipping clerk. He got along well with the men he worked with, too, and gained many friends with his sober yet cheerful disposition.

After work one day, about a month before Christmas, Ole took a stroll up the street, and in passing a saloon he thought he heard a familiar voice inside. He stopped and listened, for it resembled the voice of his friend Wang. He had not heard from him for over a year, and feared that he had taken to drinking again. But when he looked over the swinging doors, Ole did not see any resemblance to Wang in the loud-mouthed drunk. So he turned and was about to continue his walk when he heard a man ask the drunk what part of Norway he had come from. Ole stopped again to hear his answer. The drunk replied with a question of his own, "Have you even been in Norway?"

"Yes," the other voice replied, "I spent my youth there and have hopes I can go back again."

"Then, I will tell you about my home district without naming the place, so I may see if you can guess the name! But let us have a dram!" That was served and then he continued with a song native to his homeland.

"Ah, you are from Ringerike, I see!" said his companion.

"That was worth a dram," said another.

"Fill up the glasses," said a third. The bartender spoke in Norwegian and as he was filling the glasses he said that if the man from Ringerike would write down the words of the song from his home, which he had just sung, he should have all the liquor he could drink both that day and tomorrow.

Ole had heard enough to leave little doubt about who the man was, so he went in and greeted Wang, who was so surprised by Ole's entry that he looked like one struck by lightening. Ole could tell at a glance what kind of a life Wang had been living, so he did not ask any questions. Whiskers and hair had not been cut for months. On one foot was a shoe, unbuttoned, and on the other was a boot with toes showing. His coat, which should have been discarded long ago, was tightly buttoned, so that few could tell that he did not have a shirt on.

When Ole began to talk to him, Wang fell to weeping, which started boisterous laughter among his friends, and they asked if his friend might be his old "soul-saviour." If so, he had better send a message to his Heavenly Father that he needed a new coat. Wang shook his head slowly and sighed, "Oh, if I were again as I was when I left you!"

Then from the bar someone called to Wang, "Wang, bring the preacher with you so both of you may have a drink!"

"I am not a preacher, and anyway I do not drink," Ole declared.

"Not a drop more!" Wang said and shook his head vigorously.

"Come with me and perhaps you can start life over again," said Ole. "You are young and . . ."

Here Ole was interrupted by a fellow who called out, "If you won't drink, you had better get out. There's no place here for long temperance lectures. Are you going, or shall I help you?"

Ole knew better than to pit himself against a crowd of drunken men. He turned and said, "Come along."

"You are not going with him like a sheep?" one man taunted him. "Don't you want to write that song down for the bartender?"

"I'll write it sometime, but not for whiskey," replied Wang. "I've worked too long for that kind of reward already."

"Come on, boy!" said a big, burly fellow as he jerked Wang back through the door, at the same time telling Ole that he had better go if he wanted to leave with a clean face. As Ole left, he called to Wang, "Meet me in front of this 'welfare club' tomorrow afternoon at twelve-thirty."

Ole ate his lunch quickly the following day, and went to the street where many men like Wang were lying in rows. Arriving at their meeting place, he walked back and forth on the sidewalk, jeered by a few men who had seen him the night before. Wang did not come, nor was he to be found in any of the saloons. It was impossible to find out where he lived, and Ole had to hurry back to the mill at one o'clock without seeing Wang.

As he was reading the paper that night, he read the name of Nils P. Wang, one who was arrested the day before. Immediately he boarded a streetcar and went over to the police station half a mile away.

"Do you have a prisoner here by the name of Nils Wang?" he asked.

"Yes."

"May I talk to him?"

"Yes, if you can get anything out of him, he won't talk to anybody."

Ole went to the cell and saw Wang standing as if awaiting his death sentence. At the sound of Ole's voice he hurried forward to greet him.

"So I find you here," Ole said cheerfully, smiling to him through the little opening in the iron door.

"Yes, unfortunately," Wang said, unsmiling.

"But I don't have to fight anyone to get you out of here."

"That may be so, but it will take more than that to get me out of this place."

"And what is that?"

"Twenty-five dollars."

"Oh, nothing worse? I have fifty in a pinch," said Ole cheerfully.

"Yes, but it's not my money. How could I ever repay you? No, there is no hope for me anymore. I can never reform. I have no clothes and winter is soon here."

"That's true, but let's get you out of here first and talk about the rest of it later," said Ole. He went to the office and paid the fine.

He returned with the guard and Wang,

now free, went out on the street with Ole --
two utterly contrasting men as they walked
side by side.

Two hours later Wang sat in Ole's room,
dressed from top to toe. He felt better, and
began the story of what had happened to him
after Ole and he had parted. "I was a teetotaler, Ole, for one year after we separated in
Carlton, and I saved a couple of hundred dollars and bought a good supply of clothes. I
never kept anything from you in my letters. I
was weak, and I think the reason why I fell
to drinking again, after being free of the
craving for so long, was that I had to stand
alone, without you, when I was still in need
of your support. Since I saw you last night I
have not had one drip, in spite of the other
men who tried their best to make me drink. I
hope and pray that a higher power will give
me strength to withstand the temptation as
long as I live. I was able to subdue the desire
for some time, only to have violent and
uncontrollable outbreaks again, as if a vol-
cano were raging inside of me. How I wished
I could become some other sort of man, with
a good orderly life. So often I wished to
make the change, and made scores of
attempts, but they were all just like the

waves of the sea ceaselessly pounding against the rocks, rising as if they could climb to the very top, only to fall back into the turbulent sea."

Wang shared a room with Ole. About a week after his meeting with Ole he had got a job at a mill, receiving good pay, and changed so much that after eight months of sober living only a few people recognized him as the former tramp. And even though he had habitually been in a drunken stupor before Ole found him, he nevertheless had kept up with the business conditions in the city. He was certain that the bank Ole put his money in was tottering, managed by unreliable people, and would eventually fail. Ole followed his advice and took his money out, investing it in real estate in the nick of time, for three weeks later the bank did close its doors.

The next spring Wang's business sense became evident again as he told Ole of a plan. "Do you remember what I told you about the bank last fall?" he asked.

"Yes, I remember," Ole answered. "And I got good interest on the money I loaned you to get out of jail in a very short time."

"But now," said Wang, "You ought to sell

some of your lots and invest in 'Clipper' stock." The Clipper was doing a brisk business on Lake Michigan each summer, and it paid its stockholders a good dividend.

Wang's life too, began to improve when he was promoted to bookkeeper at the mill. He was well-qualified from his many years' experience in this line of work, and he filled the position to the complete satisfaction of the management. Ole and Wang became bound together more and more by mutual interests, and the reciprocal support they gave each other was largely responsible for their success. Wang was so prosperous now that he could make monthly deposits in the bank.

In the fall Ole sold his stock in the Clipper at a profit and built a large brick building on two of his lots. When the building was ready Nellie Williams and her father came to Chicago and Nellie rented one part of the building for a millinery shop. Nellie and Ole had exchanged letters, and she longed to see him again and to start herself in business. Ole established a general merchandise store in the other part of the building, after resigning his position in the mill, and he and Wang moved in. So it was that Wang became acquainted with Miss

Williams. These three became a veritable three-leafed clover, the best of friends. Wang was no longer a roving job searcher and a drunkard, but an intelligent and successful young businessman with a pleasing personality. The three had many friends now to spend the evenings with.

Miss Williams brought considerable capital with her, and with the help of her two friends she developed a lively business. Wang helped her with the bookkeeping when he had a free evening, and before his best friend realized it the association had turned into love. When Ole heard about this, he advised Wang to make a clean breast of his past, from the old country on. More than almost any other event, he hoped for their marriage and happiness. Wang followed his advice and told her everything, which however did not cool their feelings toward each other. The following Christmas they stood before the church altar as bride and bridegroom. Not many were invited to the wedding, other than Nellie's parents and their closest friends. Afterward Ole thanked the bride for all the kind things she had done for him from the very first time he saw her to this day -- from the time she knelt at his bedside, with sympathy in her heart and tears in her eyes, and unlaced the frozen moccasins from his mutilated feet, and then nursed him back to health. He continued his tribute to her before all their friends in the wedding party and spoke of their long friendship, their rescue from certain death when God had used him as His instrument of mercy and thereby he too was saved. He wished the newlyweds continued success and happiness.

After the wedding Ole lived at the home of Wang and his wife. Wang resigned from his bookkeeping job in the mill and went into partnership with Ole. The firm bore the name Haugen & Wang. The millinery shop, separated from the rest of the building, was merged with the dry goods store, and the joint enterprise became the leading dry goods and grocery store in Chicago at that time.

Chapter Twenty-Five

Plots Against Marie

It is a year now since we have heard anything from Norway. The Haugen people live better than ever before and with Ole's help they have freed themselves from debt to Bonden and still have enough money to provide themselves with a cow and a calf, a sheep and a lamb. But if there has been progress at Haugen, the opposite has taken place at Hovland. Bonden has gone deeper and deeper into debt, and his credit is no longer good. His timber lands and the income therefrom are in other hands, as is also the income from carrying mail which was taken from him after the pilfering of mail was discovered. His farm and equipment have been offered for sale at public auction many times, but each time Asle Viig, who continues to be his close companion, especially in drinking, has stepped in to help him out of his dilemma, with loans and mortgages on the property.

Asle is now of age and is possessor of three thousand dollars, which he inherited from his uncle and may do with as he pleases. It is still his hope that Marie may change her mind, when and if he buys the whole farm and equipment. When Bonden and he get together for a drink they devise plans for the best way to win her over, for it is plain that no pressure will make her yield. They must gain their end by cunning.

While Marie was serving them coffee one fall evening, her father said in an ingratiating tone of voice, "Marie! The people over at Viig have done so much for us, especially Asle. Will you not in return help the women folks with some sewing before Christmas? They have so much to do over there, and so little help."

"Yes, I can do that," she answered. She wanted to obey her father's wishes as far as possible, although she would rather have gone to prison for a few weeks. But she did not dare refuse. Asle asked her if she wanted to ride over with him now, but she excused herself by saying that she had a good deal to do, and could not come before noon the next day.

Her father took her over to Viig. He joined the men in drinking toddy, while Marie helped the women at their sewing. She remained at Viig three weeks, and although they tried in every way to make her visit pleasant, time dragged. Asle kept himself over at Hovland much of the time, to her surprise. He often brought up the subject of their engagement, but she pretended not to understand him. He also tried to arrange it so that he could spend some time up in her room, but the door was always locked and he would not jeopardize his plans by using force.

When Marie returned home she was informed that this was now Asle's home, too, for they had agreed to operate the farm together. He had moved some of his things over, along with his trotter "Sleipner" and two work horses. Thus Hovland did not become a very much better place to live in than Viig had been, and she found herself treading as if on slippery ice, with no sure foothold. Ole wrote to her often after the discovery of the forgery and mail theft, and they were well acquainted with each other's life.

At Christmas she wrote a letter to Ole and complained of the unsatisfactory situation with Asle and her father, and how they had so many drinking orgies together, night and day. She told him that soon Asle would be owner of the property, so that she would eventually have to leave her home if she had to give him a definite answer to his proposals of marriage. Two months passed, and then the most cheering letter she had ever received arrived. Ole wrote that with the situation as it was, he would return to Norway in the fall and hoped to bring enough money to establish their own home.

With renewed courage, she went about her work as happy as a bird in a tree and dreamed of Ole's return. This was the theme of conversation every time she met Randi Haugen.

One day Mother Viig came to visit Marie. She brought her some small presents and asked if she were pleased to have Asle in the house. She also mentioned that he had helped them out of their financial difficulties, and went on telling how Asle was not an ordinary boy but had the same kind feelings for her even if her father had met reverses of fortune. She added that Marie needed to

The Cotter's Son

have no fear of being jilted, for the wedding would surely take place in the fall.

"Oh, no, I am not afraid of that," answered Marie, adding "but then Asle would break his promise to Guri." She regretted at once that she had made such an impertinent remark, for Mother Viig plainly showed hurt feelings, but it could not be retracted now that it was said.

Asle was not bothering her as he had done before, but was as friendly and polite as his nature permitted. Marie became accustomed to his presence and was not quite as afraid of him as before. She even took rides with him on Sundays, or went with him to Holum church, and the people began to gossip that, "Now wealth has won its victory."

One Sunday evening when everyone was sitting at the coffee table, Bonden said amiably, "Now you must at last have given the matter sufficient consideration, Marie. Don't you think that you would be better off and have a fine future if you married Asle, than to wait for the cotter's son and have to live in want in a hovel? You must understand that you and Asle would get everything here, and with his wealth in addition he will be able to give you everything you desire.

Furthermore, it is uncertain if the cotter's son will ever come back. Even if he did, I would never consent to the marriage. I must have regard for my fatherly duty, and must not let my only child lapse into poverty when other prospects are in sight."

Asle looked at her with tense anticipation and held his breath to be certain that he would hear her answer clearly. But she did not say a word, not knowing the best way to phrase her reply. A refusal would surely anger them both, and she hesitated so long that Bonden thought he discovered a weakening in her resolve. So he repeated, "Think it over, my child! You will realize the truth of my words. You know that I am so far along in years that I will not burden myself with the active management of the farm much longer, so you will do the best by me also by permitting everything to go on unchanged. You know that I have had some setbacks and have incurred some obligations, so both you and I, I am sorry to say, must leave this home and farm if you say 'No' to Asle!"

"May I have a month to think it over?" she answered after a long pause. "I am between the bark and the wood. God knows that I want the best for us both."

It was a gentler answer than they had expected, and the time was granted.

On a Saturday evening in September, Marie went over to Haugen and had a confidential conversation with Torkil, whose advice she sought on how to answer Asle's proposal. She had not received any letters of encouragement from Ole in seven weeks. Downhearted and tearful, she told how difficult it was to be friendly with Asle, so she would not be scolded and reprimanded by her father. In situations such as this she used to have the protection of her mother, but now, lonely and deserted, she saw no hope. Except for the thought of Ole, she would often have given up in despair. She had not slept a single night through for a long time; either her thoughts drove away her sleep, or she was kept awake by the pounding on the table by the card players in the living room below.

"Things are now so changed at home," she said to Torkil. "My mother's bed and room are now occupied by Asle. Instead of her hymnbook, a deck of cards lie on the table, and under the pillow where I often found mother's prayerbook I now find an empty bottle. No longer do I hear prayers, but instead vile oaths may be heard in the still night from her bedroom after the card games are over."

Randi was expected home from the saeter, but Marie did not dare to wait any longer for it was eleven o'clock already. She went home, and when she reached the top of the steps she discovered that she had forgotten to lock her bedroom door before she left. But when she found everything her fears subsided. It was very dark in the room, and she lit a candle to read Ole's letter and look at his picture, as she did every night before going to bed. Then she snuffed the light and tried to sleep.

A few minutes later she noticed a movement under the bed, and thinking it was the dog she got up, went over to the door and called, "Come here, Trofast!"

In response, a man unsteady on his feet, and not the dog, answered her call with an impudent laugh.

Her first impulse was to shriek, but gathering courage she said, "If it is you, Asle, you will have to leave at once because it is very improper for you to be here at this time of night."

"Yes -- Yes --" Asle's voice sounded thick and unpleasantly familiar to her, coming out from the darkness of her room. "You may say what you like, but I am your betrothed. It's Saturday night, so you should let your lover be with you for a little while. That's customary here in the valley, and everywhere. Let me just talk to you about the wedding."

"We can do that in the morning just as well," Marie said coldly.

"No," answered Asle. He sat down on a chair and drew Marie down on his lap. "Your time for thinking is over. The question must be answered tonight whether you belong to me or not."

"No, for goodness sake, leave me in peace tonight! Tomorrow I will talk with you when father is home."

"Tomorrow would be cheating. Either now or never!" He pressed her closer to him, and she could smell alcohol in his breath. "What is your answer!"

She knew that there could be no further postponements and so she answered, "I cannot give you what I have not myself."

"Oh, don't give me that double-talk! Answer a simple 'Yes' or 'No.' I am as good as master of this place and I don't need to cringe and beg for evasive answers any longer!"

"Well, what I mean is that my heart has been given away a long time ago, and I have nothing to give you, for I have never had more than one heart."

"To Ole Haugen, I suppose."

"That is no concern of yours!"

"All the same, I know for sure that you mean Ole, but if you don't want to be mine, I shall see to it that you shall never marry him either, and the Sigdal River shall swallow us both before morning dawns. No one will hear you. We are entirely alone here. Erick and the girls have gone to Braaten to a dance. Your father is at Viig. If you will rather take the lives of the two of us than to give up the cotter's son, you cannot expect any better."

"Yes, but ---"

"Hush! Keep your mouth shut! If you don't keep still -- do you see this? You will never reach the river alive!" He took a big knife from its brass sheath.

For a moment there was silence, and the poor girl was near fainting. She trembled so that the table she leaned on shook and the candlestick on the table swayed.

"Is someone coming?" he mumbled, and let her go, whispering. "I will be back in two minutes. Then in another two we shall drown together. That heart you have given to Ole shall rot by the side of mine in the bottom of the river. You can save yourself the trouble of crying for help, there is no one here that will hear you."

He took the key from the inside of the door and went out quietly; locked the door from the outside, and crept down the stairway listening to hear if anyone had come.

Marie opened the window, intending to call for help, but knew it could not reach her in time. So, quickly she tied a sheet to the window, took all her letters, and dropped the bundle to the ground. She then tried to find her shoes, but hearing footsteps in the stairway and knowing that she had no more time to hunt for them, she dropped from the window to the ground, with the help of the sheet. She grabbed the bundle, her whole inheritance from this once glorious home, and ran into the dark night like a ghost, clad only in her nightgown, with her long hair floating from her shoulders as she fled over the meadows.

She did not dare to go over to Haugen, for even if Torkil could save her life Asle would find some means or other to injure them, or even to try to burn the cottage. As these thoughts raced through her mind, she reached the saeter road. She ran on, even though her tender feet struck sharp stones, and only when her terror had subsided a little, did she begin to feel the painful cuts. She did not dare to follow this way either, for the saeter had been her retreat many times and Asle would be sure to look for her there. So she went into the thick spruce forest, put on her dress and shawl, and wandered on the darkness through brush and heather, without knowing where she was going other than that she always kept towards higher ground. The whole countryside lay in slumber and peace. The deep silence was broken now and then by a twig snapping underfoot.

After awhile she heard a horse coming. "I am probably near the saeter," she thought. She heard the hoof-beats clatter below with such speed and regularity that she was certain that the horse was not a stray but that someone was riding him. Fearing to be heard, she did not dare to keep on going, and sat down in the heather. The sound came nearer until the horse finally passed her close to the place where she sat. She could see sparks fly as the horse's shoes struck the rocks.

She felt safe in the blackness of night and remained motionless. Soon she noticed a rustling sound, and could distinguish a moving shape of some kind. Suppressing a shriek of fear which would have revealed her hiding place, she was startled again when something licked her hand. It was Trofast, who had followed the scent to find her. Now she knew that the rider had been Asle.

Listening to the sound of the hoofbeats, she was able to tell in which direction the saeter road lay. She forced the dog to leave her and set out in a direction leading away from the road and proceeded along a ridge. By daylight she found herself way beyond the saeter on rugged terrain where birch and pine had taken hold instead of the majestic spruce. She shuddered at the sight of blood running from the cuts on her feet, tore the silk scarf she wore on her neck into two pieces and bound up her sore feet. She continued uphill until she reached the top of the mountain, about five miles from Hovland.

Just below the highest point of the rocky formation she saw a sheltered place covered by sapling birches. After examining the shelter for loose stones that might fall on her, she crawled in and found it to be a good hiding place. The entrance was small and overgrown with grass, so it was dark inside. Pleased that she had found this cave, she went up the ridge, sat down on a hummock, and opened the handkerchief that held Ole's letters and his picture. She looked at them and at the photograph and began to cry. Birds warbled their morning songs but their cheerfulness only increased her sadness. Putting the letters in her lap, she rested her head in her hands and looked down at her bare feet. Her brown hair hung down about her shoulders, over the shawl which she clutched tightly around her.

She raised her head and saw before her the beautiful valley, which the morning sun was just unveiling before her. She could see her home and Haugen, the Holum church, Viig and even the river, where she and Ole had been boating so many times. This cheered her a little and she tried to wipe away her tears with her very wet handkerchief. Then with two pins she fastened it across her dress to dry it in the sun. Among the few things she had taken with her she found a sheet of paper with a gilt rose painted on the upper lefthand corner, on which she began to write verses to Ole.

She put the poem in an envelope, sealed

it, and placed it in her blouse. Then she gathered moss and prepared a bed in the cave and laid down to rest. Her mind at peace, she soon fell asleep; but her slumber was often disturbed by a vision in which Asle appeared with his sharp knife. She remained in the cave far into the afternoon, where she arose and went over to the other side of the ridge. Finding some blueberries there, she managed to still her hunger and returned to her hideaway to sit and gaze at the valley below just as the sun was setting behind the mountain tops, covering the valley in the shadows. Then she went into the cave again and made her bed for the night.

The next morning she was very hungry and was determined to go down to the saeter, even though her feet still pained her. A quarter of a mile away she hoped to meet Randi bringing the cows out on the meadow. The tinkling cow bells guided her to the grazing cattle, but Randi had returned to the saeter. Disappointed, Marie followed the edge of the woods cautiously, listening and looking around. Soon she came to an opening in the woods where she could see the saeter hut, with the horse Sleipner grazing inside the yard, indicating that Asle was there.

"It would be as bad to starve to death in the mountains as drown in the river," she thought, "for with berries alone I could not live very long." There were a few berry bushes where she was hiding, and she ate some of the fruit while she watched the hut. From where she was standing she could see everything that went on. Randi and Guri were cleaning and polishing the wooden milk utensils.

The dog Trofast was running about sniffing everywhere, and soon she discovered a dark object lying beside the fence. At first Marie was not sure what it might be, but when she saw a hand thrust into a pocket and come out again with a whiskey bottle, that was all she needed to know.

She continued watching the scene and eating berries until just before sunset, when the cows gathered around Randi as she scattered salt on the rock outcroppings that dotted the meadow. She saw Asle get up and go into the hut, indicating that he was not planning to go home yet. So she had to abandon all hope of meeting Randi that night and return to her hideout in the dark cave.

Very early the next morning Marie went down toward the saeter. The tinkling cow bells told her that the cattle were being let out of the corral to be driven to their grazing range, but she stayed close to the woods until Randi came. Frightened but happy to see her, Randi declared that Marie was more like one dead than alive, for with her matted hair, white face, and wild look in her eyes, she was almost unrecognizable. Marie embraced her and cried like a child, while Randi put her own course patched shoes on Marie's feet and then hurried over to the hut to get her some food. She picked up a cowbell and told Asle, who was sitting by the breakfast table having his coffee and brandy, that a bell was out of order and that she had to go out to the herd and replace it. Then she quickly picked up a loaf of bread, some butter, and a bowl of milk, without being seen, and joined Marie in the woods. While they were eating, Randi told her about Asle.

"Asle has been going back to Hovland every night, but seldom leaves the saeter before midnight. Your father is at home and keeps watch there, and will send word to Asle when you arrive. He says he wishes you no harm, but wants you to come home. He is sure that you will return soon to the saeter or to Hovland, for he thinks you don't have enough clothes to show yourself to people anywhere else."

Marie told her how near death she had been on Saturday night, and Randi advised her to remain on the mountains a few days more until the excitement had calmed down. After agreeing on a safe meeting place where Randi should leave food, they said farewell.

Marie went up on the ridge and sat there a long time. When night came she went to bed and slept well until morning. Then she went down to the spot agreed upon and found more food there than she could eat. This went on for three days and on the third day she found a thin shaving of wood in the package on which was drawn some trees with a round circle behind them. This Marie understood to mean that Randi, who could not write, would meet her at the place indicated at sunset. So she stayed in her hiding place until the sun was half hidden behind the mountain. Both Torkil and Randi came. Torkil, who was dressed in his Sunday best, told her that her father had fifty men ready to go out to hunt for her the next day. Among these were many who wanted to protect her if she were found. If she were returned to Hovland she would be mistreated again, Torkil said, and he proposed that she

The Cotter's Son

take refuge in the minister's home, for Prost Trandberg had promised her mother on her deathbed that he would protect Marie. Torkil said that he would accompany her over there that night, and Marie agreed that this was the most sensible step to take. And since she did not have suitable clothing, Torkil promised to talk to the Prost first and acquaint the family with her plight. So Marie went to the parsonage that night and was received with open arms and much sympathy. The next morning Prost Trandberg's son, now a seminary student, and a servant boy went over to Hovland to get Marie's clothing, and soon all the men were there who were to search for Marie. A keg of liquor had been promised them and this was consumed on the spot, but not until the minister's son had finished his errand and departed.

At first Bonden refused to give him her clothes saying, "The wench can come back and behave herself decently. She must remain at home." But when it was made clear to him that Marie must remain in a place where her life was not in danger, he at last packed up a chestful of clothing and sent them with the young men.

Chapter Twenty-Six

The Cotter's Son Back Home

Hovland was in financial difficulty again because the interest was due on the mortgage. Instead of letting Asle pay it this time, Bonden decided to let the matters take their course, so that when the bank forced the sale Asle could bid on the farm at a low figure, thereby bypassing some of the creditors who had third or fourth priorities, in the amount of about two thousand dollars. Asle and Bonden reasoned that anyone who was unacquainted with the real value of the place would not bid up on an estate without timber, and as for the neighbors, they knew they would abet them in their schemes. The farm was advertised for sale at public auction at Lerberg Courthouse on the seventeenth of November, just two months after Marie came to the parsonage.

As soon as Marie's poem-letter reached Ole, he began to arrange his business affairs for his return home. He sold all his lots and buildings at high prices. His two-thirds share in the merchandising business Ole sold to Wang, who received financial backing from his father-in-law. He had, therefore, more money than many realized. After saying farewells and getting the solemn promise of Wang and his wife that they would come to Norway the next summer, he left early one October morning with the best of wishes, a great deal of money, and a trunkful of American curios, on a train that would take him directly to New York.

Nothing of importance happened on the trip. Seventeen days after his departure he sighted Norway's coast again, which he had not see for four-and-a-half years. The eighteenth day he stepped ashore in Kristiania. He decided to stay there a few days to see the public buildings and famous places, but the same evening he read in a newspaper about the foreclosure at public auction of the Hovland farm, to be held on Friday of the same week. The following Monday the household goods, machinery and farm animals would be sold at auction. So Ole took the steamboat for Drammen the next morning. It was with mingled emotions that he saw this city again, his place of departure for America. He went a little way up Strømso Street, where he last saw his father, with his wheelbarrow, on his way back to Hovland, after leaving his son to face an uncertain fate in a foreign land. With deep regret Torkil had parted with his son, who he had hoped would be his comfort and help in his old age.

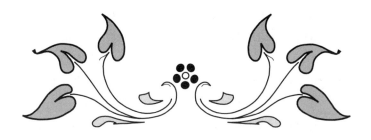

Chapter Twenty-Seven

The Cotter's Son
On Bonden's Farm

Friday, the seventeenth of November, was a cold and stormy day, and at the sheriff's farm, where the auction was to be held, it was predicted that not many would come to bid on the Hovland farm. Viig and two other farmers came shortly after noon, but by two o'clock one sleigh after another turned in to the Lerberg yard, even though the snow storm grew worse and worse. Thore Viig, wearing a big wolfskin coat, went out to meet the sleighs as they arrived, whether the occupants were acquaintances or strangers. To each one he offered a drink from his bottle.

The auction commenced at two-thirty, after the reading of the conditions under which the farm was up for bidding. Thore

Viig first bid forty-five hundred dollars, which was about half the value of the place and two thousand dollars less than the total debt. In spite of this low bid, it appeared doubtful that a better offer would be made, whereupon the sheriff stated that if the hammer should fall on Thore's bid it could not be approved at this time. At that moment a sleigh came rapidly up the road and turned into the yard, a young lad at the reins. Out of the sleigh leaped a man who hurriedly opened the courtroom door. Turning to look at the new arrival, the auction crowd saw a man who from all appearances seemed to be a city man, unknown to anyone. His great coat was made neither from sheepskin or wolf's fur, and seemed to be too curly to be cowhide. He greeted the men with a quick nod, and his sharp eyes quickly measured the gathering as he walked over to the sheriff.

"I understand the auction has already started," he said. "May I ask what are the conditions of the sale?"

These were read and revealed that the total debt on the farm was sixty-five hundred dollars, inclusive of all creditors, and that the sale would be approved immediately if an acceptable bid were made. Then the bidding began again, and the stranger called out his bid of sixty-five hundred dollars at once. Thore Viig did not dare to raise the bid, but took the stranger aside and whispered, "There are matters connected with this farm that will be influenced by the sale. My son is to marry the daughter of the former owner. It is understood that I shall buy the farm for them, so the daughter shall not need to move from her old home. And because she is motherless and her father is deeply in debt, people have sympathy for his daughter. As you have noticed, no one has opened his mouth to bid on the farm at a higher price. Therefore I hope that you too will sympathize with the situation of the poor motherless girl, brought up in comfort, who is now to see her home go into the hands of a stranger. Yours is a higher bid than the farm is worth, for it has none of the great advantages that the advertisements try to make one believe it has, and there is no timberland anywhere."

"Yes, it may be hard for the girl," answered the stranger, "but you know the saying, 'There are no brothers in card games.' If you bid over me, I shall keep up with you for awhile to put a little life in this sale. It is a dull auction when there is only one bidder."

Thore Viig and others looked goggle-eyed at the city man, and Viig raised the last bid by fifty dollars. But no sooner was this bid made, than the stranger raised the bid by one hundred dollars. Thus the bidding went on until it reached seven thousand dollars, and Thore Viig declared that he would not go a cent higher even if the girl went to the poorhouse. Then the stranger bid seven thousand one hundred dollars, and the hammer fell.

"What is your name?" the sheriff asked.

"Ole Torkilson Haugen."

"Do you have security?" the sheriff demanded.

"No," the stranger replied, and with that he took six hundred dollars out of his pocket, the stipulated amount of down payment on the bid.

While the sheriff was preparing the papers and records of the auction, Thore Viig came over to the stranger, and reaching out his hand he said, "Really, it is Ole Haugen! You have changed so much in a few years! I could give you some information about this farm deal. Buying the farm today was easy, a relatively simple matter, but I have had more experience in such things than you, and shall give you some advice. In addition to the interest due on the mortgage there is the private obligation of more than two thousand dollars due Asle, my son, due next spring, and do not think you can have this loan renewed after the way you have obstructed his plans. There is no timber or any other material to sell. I cannot understand where the money can come from, for I can just about figure out the top amount you were able to accumulate in the years you have been in America. I call your attention to this in a friendly way because I am sorry for you, both for your own sake and your parents. So I shall make you this proposition. If you will turn the deal over to me now before the deed is made ready, I shall take care of the last one hundred dollars and do the girl a kindly turn and I will be saving you from much loss and unpleasantness."

"No, I do not wish to make any changes today," Ole answered. "As far as Asle is concerned, he will have an opportunity at the next auction, if I cannot meet the obligations against it. Also, if he has the means, he probably could take care of the daughter without the Hovland farm, and I hope he has not made the farm deal a condition of marriage so that it will go to pieces on my account."

Ole got the deed that night and went to Drammen the next morning to buy the necessary furniture, bedding, and groceries. Everything was loaded on two hired sleds for the haul to Hovland. They traveled slowly with their heavy loads up over Eiker, and when they were only two miles from Hovland, Ole had to go on ahead in order to be on time for the auction on chattels at Hovland by two o'clock.

His heart beat fast when he drove past the dear familar places, the garden where a well-remembered stone lay, and the rosebushes pushing through their white blanket of snow.

No sooner had the horses stopped in front of the house than Ole heard the auctioneer's voice, "Five dollars -- two marks! Five dollars -- two marks! Let's have a better bid!"

"Hold my horse," Ole said to the boy at the door as he shouted loudly, "Seven dollars!"

"That fellow does not use two shillings!" someone remarked, while the auctioneer repeated several times, "Seven dollars! No better?"

"Eight dollars!" Asle Viig cried out. He

turned and stood on tiptoe to look over the crowd and see his old classmate.

Ole saw the chest, now up for sale, and recognized it as the one Marie had kept his letters in, as well as her clothes, ever since childhood days, and called out, "Ten dollars is what that chest is worth!"

"Fifteen dollars!" came a raise-bid from Asle Viig, so fast that the auctioneer did not have time to call it. And so the bidding went between the two until the hammer fell on Ole's bid for forty-five dollars.

"Whose bid?"

"The Cotter's Son."

"What! Does he have money for such high-priced furniture? Come here and let me see how big you are."

Ole worked his way to the table and the crowd stared, for he looked more like a well-to-do merchant than the cotter's son that they used to know. With a smile he said, "Maybe the name is somewhat incomplete? They called me that when I last was here on the farm. It is now Ole T. Haugen, and to be sure I am buying with cash."

Some kitchen utensils, and iron stove, and other articles were put up after that. When Ole came out he saw Guri standing by the fireplace smoking her clay pipe and talking to Anne Braaten. She complained that she was now without a home. She had served here more than thirty years, longer than Torsten had been the owner, and now that Asle was going to be the owner she was sure to be sent away because she had played that trick on him at the saeter. She knew she was too old for anyone to take her into service now, and she was afraid of the poorhouse.

After listening for awhile, Ole went over to her and said, "Don't be afraid, Guri! You shall be spared from moving, I shall see to that."

"But do you know Asle? He is not easy to persuade."

"Yes, I know him, but he has nothing to do with it, because now I own the farm, not Asle."

Guri continued in her own characteristic Sigdal dialect, "Who and what kind of a fine chap are you? Haven't I seen you before?"

"I am the cotter's son who so often brought you the fire to light your pipe in the years I was playing here on the kitchen floor and following you to the saeter for seven summers."

"No! Is it really you, Ole, who has grown

so big and nice and looks like a stranger! You! Maria, Maria! And you have bought the farm! How times change. I always thought from the time you were little that you had something of promise in you, and now I see right before me that I was not mistaken. I remember the many times we had fun together, how your bright eyes scanned the mountains, dancing from one peak to the other, when I would take you mountain climbing up from the saeter."

She stopped to light her pipe, giving Ole an opportunity to ask where Marie was. He made an effort to appear calm, but nevertheless showed eagerness when he inquired.

Guri told him what Marie had been through the past months, and with tears rolling down her cheeks she said, "So now I shall have you and Marie for master and mistress, something I never dreamed would happen in my old age!"

Ole had to leave her when the furniture in the parlor was up for sale. He bought most of it, with Asle helping to boost the sale prices.

The auction over, Ole asked the auctioneer to remain overnight and take care of the goods he had bought. Then he hurried out of the house with the intention of going to the parsonage, but as he stepped out of the door he became aware of the bright light in a window of the Haugen cottage, which seemed to beckon him to come over. It was half a mile to the parsonage, and the night was dark, so he decided to be guided by the light and went back to the auctioneer to get help to carry his heavy luggage over to Haugen.

He met two burly men standing on the steps talking and drinking from a bottle, which they hurriedly put away. One of them said, "Are you taking your things with you tonight and decorate over at Haugen, or will you be a cotter's boy and take your place on a stool?"

"The stool will do for me," said Ole. "I shall take my trunk and leave the rest until morning."

"So, that's what you think! But let me tell you I am going to throw every bit outside the door, for now I am the master here!"

Asle had the mistaken idea that his father, who had not yet returned from the auction, had purchased the farm.

"You are no more master here than any other stranger, I believe," Ole retorted. "Or are you by any chance married to Guri and want to remain on the place as a cotter?"

"So you think you can insult me also," roared Asle. "I shall quickly tame you, you d---- cotter's son," he added and drew a shiny dagger from its sheath and waved it before Ole.

"No, I won't wrangle with you," said Ole. "I'm really a peaceful man, but you two fellows are not to be fooled with," and he leveled two revolvers, one in each hand, at the pair.

Asle turned pale and backed away, "Well, I'll be ----! He really has guns too," he whispered to his companion, Torsten Hovland.

Torsten seemed to be a little braver. He tried to talk to Ole but everything he said was too incoherent to be understood because of all the liquor he had imbibed. Ole thought it not worth listening to and went in. Inside he met Erick for the first time since he had left, and he clasped the servant's hand warmly. In a few minutes they were on their way to Haugen with the luggage. Ole glanced through the window and saw his family at their supper table.

He said goodbye to Erick, thanked him for his help, and sat down on his trunk to let the family finish their meal undisturbed. He watched his mother carefully serve the food, while childhood memories surged through his mind. After an hour he managed to get control of himself and went in to meet the family he had not seen for more than four years.

Many tears were shed at the reunion, as on Ole's departure so long ago, but this time they were tears of joy. No one thought of bed that night, for all had so much news to tell. Ole's trunk was taken in, and out of it came dress material, handkerchiefs, gloves, books, and many other things, for everyone. The happiness in the little home that night was indescribable.

When the auction was resumed the next morning, Ole bought the whole herd of cattle, all the machinery and tools of every king, the horses and harnesses, with the exception of "Blakken," and the long sleigh. These were bought by a relative who gave them to Torsten. No one else bid on them, for the motive was understood.

At two o'clock the auction was over and all went home, except some very boisterous farm boys and Torsten Hovland and Asle Viig. Their noisy brawling continued as they went into the sitting room, and did not stop until Ole and Guri came in with a boiler of hot water between them.

"Gentlemen, will you please leave the room! We wish to clean up the place as soon as possible," Ole said.

At that Torsten and Asle roared and cried out, "Who has hired you to wash or work here on this farm? Take the scrap you have bought with you and go, and see to it that you get out, or we shall show you who shall leave the room!"

"Let me inform you, Torsten, you are the former owner of this farm. I have bought the farm. As evidence I have here the deed. You have two minutes to get out, and I hope you realize what is best for you! If you do not, I will be compelled to use other means."

The farm workers left, for this was none of their concern, while Torsten and Asle whispered to each other and began to move their purchases out very slowly and sullenly. When this was done, Asle called to Ole, who had opened the windows and was scrubbing the dirty floor with all his might, "If you have gotten in my way and have got the farm away from me, I swear that I shall squeeze you next spring. I still think I have better claim to the farm than you do!"

"I am not worrying about tomorrow," Ole replied, "even though you are in league with the devil and draw courage from liquor. The devil must yield to Him Who has protected me before and surely drunkeness cannot compete with abstinence, nor a dagger with a revolver!"

"You shall never get my permission to wed my daughter," Torsten cried. "Try, and you will find me standing in your way."

"I am no longer obligated to ask you, for she is no longer eating your bread, and furthermore she is of age and can do as she pleases."

And so the clash ended, and Torsten and Asle and Blakken headed down the road to Viig.

The Cotter's Son

Chapter Twenty-Eight

A Happy Meeting

In the afternoon of the following day, Prost Tandberg, sitting by his office window, saw two men in a carriage coming up the lane. The horse looked familiar, perhaps it was Torsten Hovland's big gray trotter, but he was not sure. As they came nearer he saw that the two men were Torkil Haugen and a stranger.

The stranger came straight into the office, and the pastor courteously asked him to be seated on the sofa.

"May I ask if a girl by the name of Marie Hovland is staying here?" the stranger asked.

"Yes, poor girl, she has been here a couple of months. She has been indisposed the last few days. One cannot expect anything else after her many troubles this fall, and particularly these last days. First there is the sale of her farm home, and yesterday all the household goods and farm equipment were sold. Perhaps you are familiar with this affair if you are acquainted locally."

"Yes, I know of her misfortune, and as I know her from her happier days, I have much sympathy for her and should like to have a talk with her."

"I do not know that she wishes to talk to anyone today. She has shied away from people since she came here, although she has done no wrong. But as her mother died nearly three years ago and her father is given to carousing, she is, you might say, a homeless orphan. In view of her early life of plenty one cannot wonder at her present depressed mind and her loneliness. It pains me to see her wander around the churchyard in the evening moonlight, to visit her mother's grave and read some old letters and sob pitifully. It would touch the hardest heart to see her there."

"If you would go up to her and ask her, I am sure she will come down. I have some information for her that she will like to hear."

"May I ask your name and I will go and

talk to her about it?"

"My name is Haugen."

"Did you come from Drammen?"

"Yes, I left Drammen Saturday."

The minister went up the stairs quietly, so Marie did not hear him, she was singing a most doleful song and although her voice was low, the minister caught some of the words, expressive of the deepest unhappiness.

Rapping at the door, he went in and found her at her sewing. "There is a very nice gentleman in my office who is asking to see you," the pastor told her.

"Oh please excuse me this time," Marie begged. "I am so weak and tired that I am unfit to meet a stranger."

"Have you not had any dinner today? I did not see you in the dining room."

"No, I could not eat a thing. My heart is so heavy that there seems to be nothing that can cheer or put life in me, however much you and our family try to help me."

"We are not doing any more than is our duty," said the minister. "No effort shall be spared to restore you to health and spirit. I am sorry that you are so discouraged. You must try to gather strength, for the person you are waiting for will certainly come if God so wills. You may yet have your best days to live!"

She did not answer, and tears fell on her sewing. At last the Prost said, "I am afraid the stranger will tire of waiting, so I must leave you. Shall I say that you feel too weak to talk to him today? He seemed to be a good, kind man, and he said that he had news you would be glad to hear. He might be acquainted with Ole Haugen or have a message from him. Let me see -- he said his name was Haugen, maybe --"

"Oh, it's Ole!" Marie interrupted him and jumped to her feet, tottered and fell back in a chair, her breast heaving with deep breathing. With a slow, shaking voice she said, "Please steady me! It is too much for me now, how can I really see him?"

The white-haired old man, whose pulse also beat faster now, took her by the arm and helped her downstairs. He opened the door to his office, and saw the visitor sitting in deep thought on the sofa. She drew back, and in her tear-filled eyes one could have read her anguished thought, "I have deceived myself!"

Then the stranger rose and an old familiar smile spread over his face.

"Ole!" she cried out in a trembling voice, and tore herself from the supporting arms of the minister to receive Ole's embrace. Both stood silent and motionless; the most touching scene the minister had seen in his long experience.

Soon they were seated on the sofa, and when the Prost looked at Marie again he was surprised to see the great change that had come over her. She smiled back at him.

The minister commented on how much Ole had changed, even to be unrecognizable to him. He asked Ole to consider himself as a guest, and to come in to meet the family and stay overnight. Ole excused himself and thanked them, but said that he had come for an announcement of marriage. He turned to Marie and said, "If it is your wish and desire?"

"You must know that," she answered simply.

Torkil was called in and the Prost recorded the banns, whereupon Ole place a five-dollar bill on the table, where seven years ago he had put another fateful five dollars. The Prost looked at Ole and the five dollars, coughed as if to make some remark, but confined it to, "Thank you!"

"The five I placed here seven years ago contributed much to my material success, may this one bring spiritual good fortune," said Ole.

"Yes, that we shall believe and pray for," said the minister as he took both by the hand and added, "I hope that He who has led you and guided you to this place will not forsake you; that your paths may now be over smoother ground -- for remember His goodness in bringing you together and giving you solace on a thorny road."

"Come home with me," said Ole to Marie, "I have a horse outside."

She did not need to be asked twice, for the home which she had in mind was the Haugen place. She had wished many times that she could have a chance to stay there. She would have liked to go there even if she had to walk all the way on aching feet, as she did when she fled up the mountain, just as long as Ole was by her side.

She dressed in a hurry and returned to the sitting room with Ole, and thanked everyone for their exceeding goodness and sympathy. Then she left happily with Ole, who wrapped her in the bearskin robe with him, and the big gray horse trotted off to Hovland.

The Cotter's Son

Ole slowed up the horse a bit and smiled over to Marie as they drove by the garden corner, but the sight of it only seemed to make her sad.

They stopped at the entrance to Hovland and Ole gestured to his father to help take care of the horses. As they stepped out Ole offered his arm to Marie. But she did not move, saying, "I thought you said you were going home! Oh dearest, go with me to Haugen! I am afraid, for father and Asle Viig must now be here alone."

"No, neither of them is here now. The only one you find here now is the hired girl."

She looked at him doubtfully, but took his hand while he led her up the steps. He opened the door to the parlor with these words, "Don't be afraid to go in at Hovland. It is your home again. I have bought the place, and what you find in the house also belongs to us."

Her eyes fell on the chest, and she saw everything as before in the parlor, with some new articles added. After standing silent with admiration, she turned to Ole, looked into his eyes, and said, "I thank you from the bottom of my heart, but words alone cannot express my happiness."

"Yes, your words are more than enough, your happiness shall be my reward. And this is only the interest on the five dollars you gave me for my confirmation."

She stood quiet and thoughtful for a long time. At last she said softly, "I see that God has always had His hand on the helm."

"Let us thank Him who alone deserves our thanks," answered Ole.

They knelt together, arm in arm, by the sofa. There was no sound, but the beating of their hearts swelled into a hymn of praise and thanksgiving. The evening sun was setting behind the Sigdal Mountains, and cast its golden rays over the landscape and through the windows of the home to rest upon the pair kneeling there, as if to say, "Welcome, and happiness in the home of your childhood." Such a scene would challenge a master's brush.

Torkil went back to Haugen and soon returned with the whole family. Ole went to the front door and asked them to "come in this way!"

When they were seated in the house, Ole continued, "If you now wish to trade the cottage for a place at Hovland, and make this your home, you may do so. Both of you have worked here enough to deserve to call it your home. The cottage at Haugen, where I was born and have had so many a night's sweet sleep, shall be cared for and so also the spot of ground on which it stands with its beautiful flowers. The forget-me-nots that smiled to me that morning four-and-a-half years ago, as if asking me not to forget them, shall be tended."

Then glancing at Marie and speaking to his parents, he added, "You will treat Marie as your daughter and I do not doubt that you will do all you can to make up for the loss of her parents."

Guri came in and greeted Marie and the Haugen folks, wishing them a hearty welcome, and announced the evening meal. They gathered around the table, with joy reflected from every eye.

Then the door opened to reveal an unexpected guest -- Torsten Hovland, the man who had lived his whole life there. He was sober and seemed depressed. He bid good evening in a low voice and sat down on a chair near the door. Ole asked him if he would join them at the table, but he shook his head, and sat silent while the others were eating. Then, when the meal was finished he rose and went over to Marie, took her by the hand and said, "Can I ever expect forgiveness from you? The way I treated you, you might now have been dead and in your grave like your mother, if another and better Father had not held His protecting hand over you. As you sat there by Ole's side I recalled the words of the Prost at your confirmation, 'The Lord's ways are not our ways.' Now I have come here to confess and ask your forgiveness, although I do not deserve it." He looked at Ole, still holding Marie's hands as she wept.

"Asle and I had agreed between us to get you out of our way and burn this place to the ground. All day I have regretted it, yet dared not withdraw because Asle was my protector and Viig my only shelter. The time was set for tonight. 'Whom God will protect is free from harm' or this whole building and all in it would have burned to ashes before morning. But what happened? Early this evening, Sheriff Bye came and took Asle away in handcuffs, after Einar Holst had confessed that he had received one hundred dollars from Asle Viig to set the saeter hut on fire three years ago. There will now be a new trial. I was freed from my pledge to Asle, but my conscience would not give me peace until I came here to talk with you. God bless you and your life together. Never again shall I be the cause of any harm to you."

He took them both by the hand as he said these last words, and tried to hide the tears that filled his eyes as he turned to go. "You have my forgiveness and no doubt Marie's also," said Ole, deeply moved, "and you shall for her sake be welcome here. You may consider this your home on condition that hereafter you will not drink. If you do abstain from liquor, you may stay here on an equal footing with my parents."

He thanked them but said that he had to remain at Viig a few days, and after that would visit a cousin farther up the valley. Then upon his return he would consider the conditions that would permit him to stay on the farm that had been the home of his father and grandfather.

"Perhaps if you will read the verses your wife gave you on her deathbed, you may return a happier man," said Ole. Torsten bowed deeply and left the house.

Ole and Marie often talked about how good it seemed to have received her father's consent and blessing before the wedding, and how happy they would be if he came back and really would stay sober during his last days.

Early one morning a couple of weeks before Christmas Erick came and wanted to talk with Ole. Ole went outside with him, wondering why he looked so frightened.

"Bonden has had an accident, but I would not say anything on account of Marie," Erick said when they were outside. They hurried to the stable, where Ole could distinguish in the twilight a horse with sleigh and driver. The horse was "Gamleblakken," which apparently had obeyed an urge to get back to his old home when Bonden was driving up from Sand the evening before and had fallen into a stupor from too much liquor. Since Bonden was unable to direct the animal, Blakken had passed by the Viig gate and continued on his own to Hovland, with his master in the sleigh.

The trampled snow showed that Blakken had been standing a long time outside the door at Hovland waiting for his master to get out of the sleigh and for Erick to come and put him in the barn. As nothing happened, the horse had taken upon himself to go to the stable door, where he stood with head drooping while Torsten still held the reins, immovable as a statue.

Ole went to the house to tell Marie what had happened. Then they headed Blakken the other way, and for the last time he brought the master to the door. There were indications of life when he was carried up the steps and into a bedroom, but before Dr. Lange came it was all over. Torsten's last words were heartrending cries for "One more dram! Water! A new deck! The game's up!"

* * *

One Sunday in the middle of December spruce branches were again spread over the snow on both sides of the road from Hovland. The sky was dark, no birds sang, instead a solemn funeral hymn was heard as eight men carried the coffin through the door. Only a few men and women dressed in black made up the group of mourners, and among them was a young woman supported by a young man who sought to console her.

As the cortege moved south toward Holum Church, the bells tolled as before, but to the listeners they did not seem to have the note of hope that they had three years ago when Gunhild was borne to her last resting place.

* * *

Christmas has come and Marie and Ole sit happily side by side in Holum Church. Next they are standing before the altar, hand in hand. The brief ceremony over, Prost Tandberg says, "Amen."

When the bridal couple came out of the church, "Halte Per" met them with a letter in his hand. He was very frail now, but he smiled broadly, and looking up at Marie he said, "Will you now accept a little Christmas present from me, also?"

He gave her the letter and limped away, a little slower than before.

When they arrived home they read the letter.

Dear Marie,
The time has come to reveal a secret, according to your mother's wish. Torsten Hovland was your

The Cotter's Son

step-father; I your real father. I served at Lie seven years when your mother was a girl. We learned to know and love each other and were engaged, but when we wanted to marry and needed her parents' consent I received instead my discharge from the farm and I was ordered never to show myself there again.

I enlisted in the army, went into battle, and was wounded, but this was not so painful as the suffering I had known after leaving Lie. Later I returned to my native valley where I have lived in a hut away from the world, on a small pension and on the game which God provided in the woods.

I received a ring from her before I was forced to leave, and herewith I send it to you, my daughter, as I am now ready to leave for another home. I also bought a ring for Gunhild with my last year's salary at Lie. But when I slipped back to Lie one evening in secret to give her the ring, she had been taken away to Hovland, there to suffer until God took her away.

I saw her, and she me, seven Christmases in Holum Church, but I talked to her only once after we parted. She declined to take the ring, saying that it might violate worldly law, but expressed the wish that it might rest on her breast after death. That wish I was not permitted to ful-

fill. It lies on top of the cover, but eventually it shall reach its place.

A happy life, Marie! Pray and have faith. We shall meet in heaven where we will renew the ties which the world with its prejudices denied us, where it is not a question of gold and silver, hundreds or thousands, no talk of hours or years, but complete rejoicing and happiness in eternity.

Your father,
Peder Olson

Marie and Ole sat a long while together looking at the letter and the ring that had brought such news to them. The following day, the second day of Christmas, they drove up to the hut to bring Halteper home, so that he could live with them. They did not take him with them, but -- in a shroud. They found him lying in bed with his hands clasping a hymn book. An inscription on the inside cover read, "Remembrance from Gunhild Lie."

The ring, which bore the same inscription as the hymn book, was placed on his right hand and followed him to the grave.

Thereafter, Ole and Marie lived a most happy life at Hovland with Ole's parents, his two sisters, and his brother. They also were blessed with sons and daughters.

Ole bought back the Hovland forest, and there was greater prosperity than there had ever been before. And soon it began to be talked about that Ole should be elected to represent Buskerud, the local political district, in the Storting (legislature).

To this day may be seen a large marble memorial in Holum churchyard, one side dark gray and the other side snow white. No preacher has ever come to Holum Church who has been able to move people so deeply as the gravestone, and it is said that he who designed it has done more good with it than a hundred ministers or lay preachers. On the dark half is engraved in black letters the following:

Beneath this stone rest
the earthly remains
of
TORSTEN PEDERSEN HOVLAND
Born 15th of January 1801,
died 11th of December 1853
Alcohol brought him here
before his time.

And on the snow-white half is engraved the following:

Here lies
GUNHHILD SVENSDATTER HOVLAND
Born at Lie the 3rd of April 1810
Died a martyr at Hovland
26th of January 1851
Rest in peace!
Blessed be your memory.
Loved and missed.
The savings bank erected this memorial.

Afterword

About the Author
Hans Andersen Foss

The Cotter's Son has been called one of Norwegian literature's greatest successes, one of the most important popular literature books in Norway's emigration literature, and the most popular Norwegian-American novel.

Its author, Hans Andersen Foss, was born November 25, 1851, at Vikersund in Modum, which is near Oslo. He left for America at the age of twenty-six in 1877. By the time he died in Minot, North Dakota, in 1929, he had written six novels and several poems and short stories. But today, nearly seventy years later, Foss and his literary works are much better known in Norway than America.

An obvious explanation for this is that his books were written in Norwegian. This has made his work more accessible to Norwegians over the years than to readers in America, where the number of Norwegian-Americans who know both languages declines with each passing generation. The only other Foss novel to be translated into English is *Den Amerikanske Saloon -- The American Saloon* (1889), done by by J.J. Skjordalsvold and published under the title *Tobias: A Story of the Northwest*.

Norwegian writings about Foss focus more than American writings on the author's childhood and the personal and financial problems that contributed to his decision to emigrate to America. Translations of two significant writings about Foss are reprinted in this book, one by Liv Kristin Asheim, from the 1984 edition of *Husmannsgutten*. The other is by Odd-mund Ljone in a January 1952 article in the *Nordmanns-Forbundet* magazine.

During his early years in America, Foss worked on farms, railroads and as a teacher in Minnesota and Wisconsin. He settled in Portland, in North Dakota's Red River Valley, in 1884. His brother, Halfden, also settled there, and remained in the area to become a longtime clothing store owner in the nearby town of Hatton. Foss completed his first novel, *Husmanns-gutten -- The Cotter's Son*, during the winter of 1884.

Husmannsgutten made its first appearance in the *Decorah Posten* on December 3, 1884, (Issue number 332). In each issue through April 22, 1885, (Issue number 342) the left hand one-third of page two ran in succession two or three of the book's twenty-eight chapters. The publication had small type and page dimensions that by today's newspaper standards are large (twenty-seven-and-a-half inches high by twen-

The front page of the Decorah-Posten on December 3, 1884, the issue containing the first installment of H.A. Foss's Husmandsgutten, which appeared on page two. (From the archives at Preus Library at Luther College, Decorah, Iowa.)

ty-one-and-a-half inches wide). Placed around it were other articles and advertisements for products like glycerine, iron tonic, steamer lines and an American dictionary.

Following the success of *The Cotter's Son*, Foss entered the newspaper business himself, owning publications in Portland, Grand Forks and Hillsboro, North Dakota, and Moorhead and Minneapolis, Minnesota, which he used to promote his temperance views and his Populist politics. While living in Minneapolis, his support of Governor John Lind brought him an appointment to the Minnesota Grain Inspection Department in 1899. He and his family then lived in Duluth, Minnesota, where he began

The Cotter's Son

working for the Atwood-Larson Grain Company. In 1907 he moved his family to Minot to become the company's dealer representative. He was influential in organizing farmers' elevator companies in Minot, Surrey, DesLacs, Lone Tree and Berthold. Eventually Foss became a part-owner of the Atwood-Larson Grain Company.

While in North Dakota, Foss continued to write and remain active in state politics. *Kristine Valdresdatter* holds the distinction of being the only Foss novel to be made into a movie, which was shown throughout Norwegian America in 1933.

Foss was an early supporter of North Dakota's Non-Partisan League when this farmers' movement was formed in 1915. But a short time later he turned against the movement and left the League. In 1921 Foss supported Ragnvold Nestos, a Republican, in his successful bid for governor, and later Foss's name appeared on the North Dakota ballot as a candidate for Congress from the Independent Party. He also strongly supported the successful campaign to include prohibition in the North Dakota constitution. Governor Nestos remained a close friend and was a pallbearer at Foss's funeral, along with Minot's mayor, A.J.H. Bratsberg.

Foss died at the age of seventy-eight, and his obituary listed as survivors his wife, Inger, and five children, Clarence, Harriet, Mabel, Inga and Herman.

Foss was not the first or only author to write novels centering around cotters' sons. Among the other novelists were Bjørnsterne Bjørnson, one of Norway's best known writers and public figures, whose *En Glad Gut -- A Happy Boy* was published in 1859, and Ole

Shown above are six of the sixteen editions of Husmannsgutten that have been published since 1884. These books are from the collection of the Vesterheim Norwegian-American Museum in Decorah, Iowa.

Buslett, another Norwegian-American author, whose *Fram -- Forward* was published in 1880. They have similar plots to *The Cotter's Son.* However it is Foss's novel that remains the most popular.

A thorough profile of Foss and his works is written by author Orm Øverland in *The Western Home: A Literary History of Norwegian America,* published in 1996 by the Norwegian-American Historical Society. He calls *The Cotter's Son* the most popular Norwegian-American novel, and analyzes its continuing popularity:

"But there is good reason why Foss achieved popularity with his version while Buslett did not. Both concocted improbable plots, both wrote wooden dialogue and both, influenced but barely inspired by Bjørnson, gave their characters poorly written verse to sing at inappropriate times. Buslett, however, shows no interest in character: in his seventy-five pages, compared to Foss's 278, he merely gives a rough outline, telling what happened to his characters rather than letting his readers get to know them so that they could take interest in them. The basic theme of both is America as a land of success for the diligent and lucky, but while Foss's transcending message is one of social criticism, Buslett's is one of romantic idealism: his hero is a model for youth who want to go 'Forward.' "

As a cotter's son himself, his early life experiences gave Foss the insight to portray this life in *The Cotter's Son* with such poignancy that Liv Kristin Asheim has called the book the "*Uncle Tom's Cabin* for Norwegian cotters."

Others have called Foss the "Norwegian-American Bjørnson," because like Bjørnson, Foss's work portrayed a belief in social progress and perfecting humanity.

That is not to say Foss's work is considered by critics to be of the same high literary quality as Bjørnson's writings. The popularity of Foss's work is its appeal to a mass audience of readers.

Norwegian poet and critic, the late Johan Falkberget, explained this appeal, writing that "*The Cotter's Son* is one of few books before which the critics stand helpless -- for it concerns itself with the eternal power of human nature, that which might be called 'the dreams of life.' "

From his childhood as the son of poor farm work-

This monument marks the gravesite of Foss and other family members at Rosehill Cemetery in Minot, North Dakota.

ers, his early struggles and setbacks, his immigration to America and his contributions as a journalist, novelist, politician and businessman, the life of H.A. Foss was truly a remarkable one. People of Norwegian heritage throughout the world can proudly claim Foss as one of their own -- a man whose life made a difference in many ways.

In contrast to his impressive accomplishments, the last sentence in his obituary in the *Minot Daily News* on the day of his death, July 9, 1929, reflects a modesty and reticence that is characteristic of many Scandinavians: *"Of a retiring nature, Mr. Foss is remembered by his many Minot friends as one who did not often speak of his achievements."*

The Cotter's Son

Husmannsgutten -- Uncle Tom's Cabin for Norwegian Cotters

By Liv Kristin Asheim

This is the English translation of the article that appeared as the Afterword to the 1984 printing of *The Cotter's Son*. It is reprinted with permission from author and educator Liv Kristin Asheim and Aschehoug Publishing Company, Oslo.

This edition of *The Cotter's Son: A Story from Sigdal* is the sixteenth edition in this country. It was previously out in 1959, and in the 1960s it was published as a serial in small Norwegian newspapers. In the 1950s it and another novel by the same author, *Kristine Valdersdatter*, were translated into New Norske. The dust jacket of the 1957 edition of *The Cotter's Son* says this book sold 100,000 copies, among the largest number of any Norwegian book that has ever come out.

It is interesting to note how *The Cotter's Son* came to be. In 1883 the Norwegian newspaper *Verdens Gang* had a debate over the cotter system.

Norwegian-American H.A. Foss wrote an article about the conditions under which cotters live, but it was too long for the newspaper. This article he later rewrote to become his first novel, *The Cotter's Son*.

The Cotter's Son was first published by the near-bankrupt Norwegian newspaper in Iowa, *Decorah-Posten*, in 1884. There it proved to be very successful, and the editor credits *The Cotter's Son* with the honor of more than rescuing the newspaper. Later the novel came out in book form with the initiative of the same editors who paid for its cost. In 1886, it was published for the first time in Norway by O Steens Bogtrykkeri in Drammen. In our country the book has been so popular it has been read until only shreds remained.

The author hit the bull's eye with *The Cotter's Son*. Norwegians in America detested the poverty conditions of the common people and the old Norwegian social structure. Norwegian-Americans themselves had abandoned the old country and had experienced a more developed society at close quarters. And in Norway the cotter system was close to collapsing.

The man behind the successful *The Cotter's Son* is H.A. Foss, 1851-1929. He was born in Modum. In the church book his father was registered as a cotter. Foss can remember that he had to go barefoot to church to save his shoes. His father's position probably improved during his upbringing. In 1866 H.A. Foss was confirmed. He then moved to relatives in Ringerike and opened his own country store when he was twenty-one years old. He married Marie Erikson, the daughter of the manager of Skaerdalen Bruk, a sawmill where Foss was the bookkeeper.

In 1873 Foss served his time in the military. He began to abuse alcohol and this abuse got the best of him, causing bankruptcy of his country store. He also had problems in his marriage, and he was pressured to emigrate in 1877. His wife and children remained behind in Norway. Marie Erickson later divorced Foss and she also emigrated.

Until the success of *The Cotter's Son* Foss most likely had a difficult time. He made a living doing railroad work and farm work, among others. Later he was a farm hand in the summer and a teacher in the winter. During this time he had a serious alcohol problem, but after the success of *The Cotter's Son* he became a teetotaler. In 1886 he married a woman from Valdres. From that time on he was very active in different social issues, especially those important to Norwegian-Americans.

After *The Cotter's Son*, H.A. Foss wrote *Life in the Western Home* (1886). Here he upholds a harsh judgement against the Norwegian-Americans' Christian denomination. The tendency is so coarse that the book was not well received. That same year *Kristine: A Story From Valdres* was published. The novel is a critical portrayal of folklife that especially focuses on the superstition which was alive and well among people. It is probably the least interesting of Foss's books, but it is the only one that was made into a movie. In the years after *Kristine*, Foss was very active in the temperance cause.

Norwegians were accustomed to Saturday night drinking and carousing, and encountering all the American bars implied a threat to many. Instead of drinking to get drunk once a week, they would do it often daily, and naturally, suffered the consequences. With his book *The American Saloon* (1889), Foss was blunt with a sharp attack on the forces in society that earn a living on the misuse of alcohol. Capitalism and corrupt government officials were singled out for only thinking of profit. Thus, Foss set the politics of alcohol in a large social connection, and his political commitment continued to increase in later years. In *White Slaves* the characters of Pluto, Monopolio and Schylock rule, symbols of those who had power in the capitalistic America. Society is permeated with corruption and the only thing that runs it is profitmaking. The sacrifices for capitalistic plundering are the producers: workers and farmers.

White Slaves' number one hero, Knut Rolfson, was forced to sign a contract after taking part in the American Civil War (but Foss continued to pay attention to profit making as an important motive of participating Northern states.) He is a prisoner of war and can choose between signing or death. The contract carried with it twenty years of slave work in a mine or pit. His family is informed that he is dead, and after the war was won, the corrupt country does nothing to investigate what happened to the prisoners of war. Knut is saved out of the mine after eighteen years of work by his son and the only respectable advocate among a countless number of corrupt people, Mr. Hartman. Knut Rolfson was earlier pressured to emigrate from Norway. He was of the opinion that there was more Christianity in Marcus Thrane [A labor leader and politican activist who came to America in 1864 after serving a prison term] than in the pastor, and lost therefore his position as a teacher. In America he anticipated the fulfillment of freedom, equality and brotherhood, but he now realized "that the fight between rich and poor, that I believed, the old world had monopoly, exists just as much in the new world" (*White Slaves*).

The honorable advocate Hartman said in the ending of the book, "I repeat, we have won a great victory, but until socialism sinks down as an angel of salvation over the nations, we will hear and learn about embezzlement, bribery, hypocrisy, burglary, forgery, robbery and murder" (*White Slaves*).

It should be unnecessary to point out that the author of this book has very strong radical political views. When I, in spite of this, find it necessary to emphasize this, it is because Willy Dahl [a Norwegian university professor], in his book, *Poor Reading Under the Kerosene Lamp* (1974), said that Foss belonged to a group of authors who were conservative and who "produced an acceptable conservative folk literature." Jon Flatbø and Karen Sundt, on the other hand, "were critical to the middle class society and openly voiced their support for radical forces in this society."

Karen Sundt's *Work Life* is worker friendly, but moderate and reformistic and completely pales in comparison with the socialistic war story *White Slaves*, which has a subtitle of *A Social Political Portrayal*. That which led Willy Dahl astray was probably the fact that he had read Foss's next and last book, *Valborg*, which came out thirty-five years after *White Slaves*. The ideas presented in this book are primarily the importance of preserving the Norwegian culture and language in America.

The Cotter's Son 297

Otherwise the book clearly has a conservative tendency, where socialism has a negative value, quite contrary to *White Slaves*. The explanation is simply that Foss changed his political views. His radicalism was heightened in the times around *White Slaves*, when he was very active. But in the 20th Century, the former radical editor succeeds as a businessman in the grain industry. While during the 1890s he fought against the Republicans and tried to be elected to Congress on a Populist radical platform but lost, just barely, he came to support the Republicans awhile after the turn of the century. The author of *The Cotter's Son* and *White Slaves* is in some ways not the same man who wrote *Valborg*. This should by itself underscore the necessity to be careful about generalizing regarding the tendency in an author's books. With an author who is politically radical, we should not automatically assume that his books have a radical theme.

H.A. Foss was a strong admirer of Bjørnstjerne Bjørnson. All of his novels contain quotes from one or more of Bjørnson's farm stories, and in one of them there is a discussion of Bjørnson. Here he is defended by a "positive" person, while a "negative" person attacks him for being an atheist.

What is interesting about *The Cotter's Son* is that on the surface it is the same story as Bjørnson's *The Happy Boy*. A cotter's son loves a farmer's daughter, but doesn't get her because of the class differences. After raising his social status in connection with travel away from home, the boy nevertheless gets the girl. The boy's rival is together with the girl's father and grandfather in competition.

While *The Happy Boy* has considerable literary qualities, we can hardly say the same about *The Cotter's Son*. It can safely be placed among the popular literature of the time of authors like Rudolf Muus, Jon Flatbø and Karen Sundt. When *The Cotter's Son* today, one hundred years after it first came out, nevertheless demands an interest, it is not caused by the novel's literary aspect. But the literature the people really read can give us a type of knowledge of readers and social conditions they lived under, where fine literature may not do so.

Can popular literature have a more direct connection with society than fine literature? Value and attitude fluctuate with various historical and social conditions, and it can partly explain that most of the typical popular literature has a shorter lifetime than fine literature.

What is the reason that *The Cotter's Son* became such a huge success? The action is simple, and clearly less exciting than a portion of other popular literature novels from around the same time. The portrayals of the people are flat with a clear division between the good ones and the evil. An interesting exception is Nils Wang. He tells about Ole's life history, which is similar to Foss's own, from his background to leaving Norway to his continued alcohol abuse in the United States. Otherwise, it is only the bad people who drink in *Husmannsgutten*. Wang remains as an extremely positive figure in the story. The reader gets a thorough explanation for why he drinks, and besides, Ole's sympathy and concern for him are good enough proof that he is good in spite of his weakness.

The Cotter's Son plays heavily on sentimental feeling, and the various complications create compassion rather than excitement among the readers. The poor Marie sleeps out in a cave because the evil Asle is after her. There is no limit to how great Ole's mother, presented as quite the martyr, must suffer. Readers are touched in chapter after chapter by the good persons' sufferings.

However, sentimentality is not a satisfactory explanation of the success of *The Cotter's Son*. We must not forget the story, in addition to movingly telling about the good heroes' problems in an evil world, also makes a strong attack against the cotter system as an institution. When one compares how the historians describe the living conditions of cotters from the eastern part of Norway with what Foss wrote in his book, it is clear that the description of the social background is very realistic. Cotters are portrayed as wretched as we can assume they were. Compared with Bjørnson's *The Happy Boy*, it is Bjørnson who romanticizes. He paints the reality in pink when he lets his cotters live under safe conditions and not suffer any due to material shortage. I maintain this view, even though the tenant farmer from the western part of Norway, who Bjørnson probably portrays was better off than the working cotter from the eastern part. The cotter system had its "golden age" when it was most widespread from around 1840 until the 1860s. In 1845 there were 60,000 cotters with land, and they made up sixty percent of all farm owners. For almost twenty years this number was nearly constant, with a little increase in 1850 and the early 1860s. The 1840s especially were known as a very hard time for cotters. They took part in activities of the Marcus Thrane movement that was at its height in 1851 with 30,000 members. In 1850 a cotter's commission was first established that obtained information about the conditions of cotters. The majority of the data concluded that their standing was deteriorating, going from bad to worse. Authorities realized that reforms were necessary, and in 1851 a cotter's law was adopted. This, however, had little practical meaning. Towards the end of the century the cotter system was gradually ending. This was due through, among other things, the passing from a barter economy to a money economy and the beginning of industrialism in Norway.

In *The Cotter's Son*, where the action takes place in the 1850s and 1860s, it is clear that it is the working cotters we encounter. This agrees with the fact that the action is taking place in Sigdal in eastern Norway. Torkil and Torsten have a written contract. By the 1800s a law established that it should be done that way. Torkil had work duties, and the cotter's work duties are represented in the story as follows: *Up and down the valley one could now hear the continuous pounding in time with the large piles, where the cotters got six skilling every workday to stand in the barn from four a.m. until seven p.m., pounding with full force to separate the grain from the husk.* At many places one even had to make four good brooms after seven p.m. before one could be the owner of six skilling. (1/120th of a daler, about equal to one cent).

Randi joined in the work of the farm, and Ole had to be a shepherd early in life. It was customary for the cotter's family to participate in work. In addition, Ole and Torkil handled forest work, and this was exactly the kind of work Eastern Norway cotters were asked to do in addition to their farm work. On one occasion the farmer demands the departure of the cotter's family from Haugen and that is in agreement with the fact that cotters did not have their place for a lifetime, and could easily be fired. The farmer points out the fact that the length of the contract had run out a long time ago. The cotter family was plagued with poverty and starvation and Ole feared that his parents would have to get poor relief if he didn't help them out of this oppressive position. There is a general agreement that the cotters lived under difficult conditions in an ongoing battle against hunger and with threats of needing poor assistance hanging over them. The conclusion is clear: The portrayal of cotter's conditions in *The Cotter's Son* is not exaggerated, but corresponds well with the historical accounts of this period.

Emigration to America is also written about in *The Cotter's Son*. Ole believes the cotter's system is slavery, and the only solution he can envision is to travel to America. This country was made out to be ideal in the story; there can people work to overcome poverty and need. And not only that, lucky people like Ole can be rich in a flash. The dream of America is, everything considered, another reason for this novel's popularity.

The first fifty-two emigrants left Stavanger as early as 1825. It was Cleng Peerson who opened the way for Norwegian emigration. From then until 1850, 17,000 to 18,000 people had emigrated to America, and nearly half of them left in the two crisis years of 1849 and 1850.

The years 1866 through 1915 can be called the mass emigration period. In the years between 1866 and 1900, more than sixty percent of the population left Norway. Of the European countries, only Ireland had a greater percentage of emigration than Norway. Ole must have traveled to America around the time the mass emigration started in Norway, namely 1865. His reason for leaving is escaping poverty, without any signs of oncoming betterment. He wants to prevent his parents from having to get poor assistance, and it is pretty likely that would have been their fate.

Ole returns to Norway. True enough, in 1920 there were nearly 50,000 Norwegian-Americans living in Norway who had returned. But in the 1870s, which is relevant to our investigation, this number was insignificant. A twenty-two-year-old Ole returning home just in time to buy the Bonden's farm at an auction sale is a sweet story but it is an unrealistic dream. During this time it is interesting that other literature of the same time as *The Cotter's Son* contains many stories about returning Norwegian-Americans. The returning American traveler in Norwegian poetry appears as early as 1839, in Hans Allum's play *Bonden Ebben i Fødelander eller Amerikareisen -- The Farmer Ebben in the Fatherland or the Journey to America.*

This frequent occurrence of returned Norwegian-Americans in literature can be explained by being the carrier of a certain notion. In Bjørnson's poem they are the advocates of liberalism and tolerance

and often come in conflict with the social environment. The same happens to Lona Hessel in Ibsen's
Samfundets Støtter -- The Pillar of Society.

The radical poets assessed America positively.
The view of America in *The Cotter's Son* can therefore not be used to argue that the book's ideology is
conservative.

The Cotter's Son clearly attacks the cotter system.
The effect of this attack is weaker than I think it is
meant to be, because the cotter's son is portrayed as
perfect, and also not very realistic. It is, however,
not obvious that all the readers recognize these weak
tendencies due to the lack of realism. Perhaps a
"less sophisticated" reader would be in a greater
uproar over the cotter system by reading about how
the noble cotter's family suffer under it, rather than
reading of a naturalist's portrayal of a similar environment and where weight is placed on poverty
"which depresses, demoralizes and destroys."

It would be natural to compare *The Cotter's Son*
with *Uncle Tom's Cabin*. Here the attack over Negro
slavery in melodramatic terms created a response
with readers. Black people are treated as melodramatic heroes and heroines. Their characteristics express
society's values at the time but what was brave and
new is that they are black. In this way the attack
on slavery achieves a breakthrough with the general
public. The book had an extremely strong influence
and was viewed by many as co-responsible for the
American Civil War and abolition of slavery. In *The
Cotter's Son*, it is the cotter's system that is treated
roughly and cotters are heroes. It is worthwhile to
note that there is no representative from the high

social layer of the town who is portrayed positively. The pastor places confirmands on the church floor based on how much money they have given him. Clerk Holst is so fond of money that he sets the saeter -- the mountain cottage -- on fire with the threat of murder for Asle's one hundred daler, and the judge's deputy, Carl Strøm, is the boon companion with Torsten.

In 1884 the liberals won an important victory with the establishment of a parliamentary government in Norway. After awhile, the voices speaking up for the old governmental state were silenced. A defense of the cotter system in the new society with the important changes they had on villages must otherwise be an anachronism.

The attack on the cotter system in *The Cotter's Son* was in keeping with the new times, but it must nevertheless have had a great influence. It was, after all, only twenty years since the cotter system was at its height. Besides it is very likely that it is first when a social institution is overturned that the hatred against it has its strongest articulation.

In his book Foss takes a stand for the old society's underclass. The author of *The Cotter's Son* is the first to portray the cotter relationship in Norway with cotters as heroes and farmers as villains. His attack on the cotter system represents with that something new in Norwegian literature. This makes the book still interesting to readers even one hundred years afterwards. The story is, in spite of all its shortages, a part of our culture in heritage, and gives a believable picture of the cotter's living conditions in the last century.

The author of *The Cotter's Son* can be viewed as an active person who wants to advance a position, not having the means to create fine literature and therefore making use of prevailing popular literature. Perhaps such a person was more easily heard in the 1880s and 1890s than in our days. Did more radical elements exist earlier than what we find today? If the answer is yes: Can this have a connection in that we had a stronger underclass-consciousness at that time, which then led to a greater demand for "radical popular literature?"

Liv Kristin Asheim earned her master's degree in 1980 in sociology, history, Spanish language and literature, and Nordic language and literature. This article was based on her master's thesis, which was a comparative study between Foss's Husmannsgutten and Bjørnson's En Glad Gut.

Asheim lives in Oslo with her husband, Harald Olsen, and two children, Anders and Ingrid. She now teaches the Norwegian language, along with an orientation on literature, history and general social life in Norway, in a school for adult immigrants, political refugees and asylum seekers. Some of her students have also been Americans with Norwegian ancestors.

The Cotter's Son
and its author:
A 100-year memory

By Oddmund Ljone

This is the English translation of an article that
appeared in Norway's *Nordmanns-Forbundet* magazine in January 1952. The late Oddmund Ljone
was a Norwegian author and journalist. Reprinted
with permission from *Nordmanns-Forbundet,* Oslo.

Well, no popular literature book in our emigration
history has meant as much and played such a role as
The Cotter's Son. It is known among hundreds of
thousands of people, read forwards and backwards. It
has brought forth smiles and tears and brought the
author's name to hundreds of thousands. And today
it is once again published. It is one of the few books
written in Norwegian America which also has
become a "best seller" here at home.

There is no reason to hide that *The Cotter's Son* is
an insignificant book in terms of its literary value
and that H.A. Foss is an author who cannot be considered a great artist. Nevertheless he defends the
position he has achieved with many. And even

though the critics may describe *The Cotter's Son* as a "bad" novel, one cannot deny that it has been read for seventy years -- and that it is still being read to this very day. And then it remains a debatable question how it has achieved this.

Last fall -- November 25, 1951 -- was one hundred years since Hans Andersen Foss was born in Modum. His parents were poor operators of a small farm, hard workers and modest people who never had any surplus of this world's material goods. The son had a stronger sense for life's possibilities. He was interested in business, and was also filled with an almost greedy desire to devour books. As soon as he reached adulthood, he became a store clerk and bookkeeper, and right after reaching his legal age he started his own business. However, this venture failed, and in 1877 he set course for America.

Hans A. Foss found that his road to America was not covered with gold; he fully experienced the fate of the emigrant. He settled in the Red River Valley, on the prairie where Norwegian emigrants were breaking the soil. He took whatever handyman chores were available and the financial situation was tight. But he was an observant kind of man, interested in what happened around him. Writing had always interested him, so he started to correspond with the Norwegian newspaper *Verdens Gang*. An article he wrote about the conditions of tenant farmers was too long for the paper, so he reworked the article to become a novel -- *The Cotter's Son*.

It was hard to find a publisher; the manuscript was promptly returned. But down in Decorah, Brynild Anundsen struggled with the *Decorah-Posten*. The financial situation was terrible, close to bankruptcy, and Anundsen was looking for something which could save the newspaper. He put his bets on *The Cotter's Son* and hit the jackpot. It was printed as a serial and became a fantastic success. The number of issues increased to unknown heights. Suddenly, everyone wanted the small paper. The emigrants drove for miles to get the *Posten*. At home they were fighting to be the first to read it. The serial was cut out, circulated and read until only shreds remained. Everyone had to read *The Cotter's Son*, and to be able to do so they needed *Decorah-Posten*.

And *Decorah-Posten* was saved. It got the financial foundation which made it possible to achieve the incontestable leader position the paper has to this day in Norwegian America. The paper became a preserver of Norwegian culture in the foreign country. Without it, the nationalistic characteristics and the Norwegian values the emigrants had brought with them to their new country would have been lost in little time. In truth, a valuable "byproduct" of H.A. Foss's literary work.

H.A. Foss was suddenly a great author. But Foss was also an advocate. He became a relentless teetotaler who, with his every being, worked for the temperance movement in this home state, North Dakota. His life philosophy was radical, and in the radical movement, "populism," he found support for his own ideas. He devoted all his energy to the temperance movement and gradually became a leader and trendsetter in both. In 1888, he bought *Normanden* in Grand Forks, a paper he made a spokesman for his ideas and thoughts, which seemed to gain great influence in the state. Foss always had compassion for the little people in the society, those who suffered, either under the curse of alcohol or lack of money. He became their spokesman. He was a natural activist and didn't steer away from a challenge. He was tireless in his work and agitation -- that the paragraph about prohibition became part of the state's constitution was to a significant extent due to his involvement.

In 1883, he sold *Normanden* and started *Nye Normanden* in Moorhead, Minnesota. Shortly thereafter he moved the paper to Minneapolis.

However, a new time had arrived. Foss himself was away from his home state and he didn't find the elbow room he sought. New political constellations appeared, and the Populist movement became divided due to internal strife. The paper went bankrupt, and once again Foss was without resources. Also he discovered that together with the loss of prosperity and influence comes the loss of friends. A poor man always stands alone. However, he got an excellent position in North Dakota, and when he died in 1929, he was once again an affluent man.

H.A. Foss continued to write throughout his life. *Livet i Vesterheimen -- Life in the Western Home* and *Kristine Valdersdatter -- Kristine Daughter of Valdres* were great successes. In the books *Den americanske saloon --The American Saloon* and *Hvite Slaver --White Slaves* he voices his opinion of alcohol and its influence on the individual and on society as a whole. He finished the book *Valborg* shortly before his death.

What then is the reason for the fantastic success

of *The Cotter's Son?* I believe the answer to be that thousands of Norwegian emigrants living on the prairie of the Midwest recognized themselves in the book.

Those who occupied the few and in between farms usually came from poor living conditions in Norway. They had left the old country because there was no room for them there -- at least no "room in the sun." They came from small farms and tenant farms and had personal experience with the class distinction in the towns where the wealthy farmer and the government official made up the distant and unreachable tops on the steep social ladder. The youth were kept from utilizing their active spirit and ambition, its deepest root being the desire to reach "up there." But in Norway in those days there was no way "up there" for the cotters' sons. The possibility only existed in dreams and fever-induced visions. But in America the opportunities were waiting. Thousands upon thousands of young people stood on the deck of the emigrant ships and saw their fatherland sink into the sea. They weren't filled with bitterness and hatred; just a presumptuous dream of one day returning, being on equal footing with the well-to-do farmer. Yes, maybe even with the pastor and the tax collector.

The simple and naive story about the cotter's son, therefore, became a story about themselves in the way they dreamt the story could possibly be told one day. In this book they met their own bold dreams and longings. Foss did not glorify the emigrants' living conditions; he knew their fate better than a lot of people. Even though the majority may never

The Cotter's Son 311

have returned home as they had dreamt about, and which Ole Haugen got to do, America nevertheless offered compensation in their consciousness. And *The Cotter's Son* continued the dream, where they themselves perhaps had to give up due to the circumstances of life.

Foss strongly stresses the class differences of the town society; the snug potentates got their earful. Many a heartfelt laugh were quite certainly heard in the poor pioneer homes. Many a tear probably fell too, and many a head was lowered in a recognizing bow. They could see themselves. They were on common ground.

The Cotter's Son met a need, released a secret longing. Therefore it became a "great" book and H.A. Foss is a great author for his time. In this way both the book and its author became instrumental in the Norwegian cultural life in America.

And because the same dreams and same longings still reside in us, *The Cotter's Son*, one of Norwegian literature's greatest successes, still finds readers today.